Alfred William Pollard, Geoffrey Chaucer

Chaucer's Canterbury tales

The squire's tale

Alfred William Pollard, Geoffrey Chaucer

Chaucer's Canterbury tales
The squire's tale

ISBN/EAN: 9783337174767

Printed in Europe, USA, Canada, Australia, Japan

Cover: Foto ©Andreas Hilbeck / pixelio.de

More available books at **www.hansebooks.com**

THE SQUIRE'S TALE

CHAUCER'S CANTERBURY TALES

THE SQUIRE'S TALE

EDITED
WITH INTRODUCTION AND NOTES BY

A. W. POLLARD

London
MACMILLAN AND CO., Limited
NEW YORK: THE MACMILLAN COMPANY
1899

GLASGOW: PRINTED AT THE UNIVERSITY PRESS
BY ROBERT MACLEHOSE AND CO.

CONTENTS.

		PAGE
INTRODUCTION,		vii
THE SQUIRE'S TALE,		1
NOTES,		26
GRAMMAR,		40
GLOSSARY,		43

INTRODUCTION.

THOUGH so great a master of narrative poetry, Chaucer seems to have been far from proficient in inventing a plot. The merest outline of a story by another writer sufficed him, and with this given he could expand and modify, imparting fresh life to the characters, and adding humorous or dramatic touches with the utmost success. But to invent a story out of his own head seems to have been beyond him. *The Dethe of Blaunche the Duchesse*, and his charming and playful poem, *The Parlement of Foules*, are sketches too slight to be reckoned exceptions. In *Anelida and Fals Arcyte* he tried to work some of Boccaccio's materials from the *Teseide* into a new story of his own, and left a mere fragment of some three hundred lines. In the *Hous of Fame*, under the influence of Dante, he set out to compose a new Vision, and again was unable to carry out his plan. In the majority of the *Canterbury Tales* his work of translation, adaptation, or expansion can be easily traced by the help of the "Originals and Analogues," published by the Chaucer Society.[X] The genesis of the Squire's Tale has baffled investigation more than any other, and the fact that it is unfinished, that the six hundred lines which we possess leave us still at the threshold of the story, suggests that we are here in presence of one of Chaucer's rare attempts at a more or less original plot. He seems, if we may hazard a guess, to have heard or read several Eastern tales, and to have formed the ambitious project of combining them into a single story, which would have required many thousand lines for its proper development. When his invention began to fail him he set down, as if by way of notes for his own future use, some of the incidents which this great romance was to contain, and it is worth while, with the help of these lines and some earlier passages, to realize for ourselves how vast the story was to be.

(i.) It was to tell us something of the Tartar King, Cambiuscan, and of his conquests (ll. 661-63).

(ii.) The King of Araby and Ind sends Cambiuscan on his birthday feast two magic gifts for himself, a horse of brass and a miraculous sword, and two for his daughter Canacee, a mirror which would disclose any treason in war or love, and a ring enabling the wearer to understand the speech of birds. All these gifts would have to be used in the course of the story.

(iii.) By the help of her ring Canacee converses with a falcon who has been deserted by her love, and the story was to tell how by the aid of Canacee's younger brother, Cambalus (or Cambalo), this falcon—perhaps an enchanted princess—"gat hire love ageyn" (ll. 654-56).

(iv.) Canacee's other brother, Algarsyf, the eldest son of Cambiuscan, after great dangers, through which he is to be helped by the horse of brass, is to win for wife a lady named Theodera (ll. 663-66).

(v.) Another Cambalo is to fight in the lists with

Canacee's two brothers, Cambalo and Algarsyf, and to
win Canacee as his prize.

Thus we are promised three distinct love stories,
with the conquering career of Cambiuscan as a back-
ground to them, and the use of the magic gifts as a
connecting link. In the first six hundred lines Chaucer
introduces some of the characters, describes the magic
gifts, brings the first love story up to the point at which
the tale begins, and then leaves us! Two centuries
and a half later Milton in *Il Penseroso* longed for the
power to

> "Call up him that left half told
> The story of Cambuscan bold,
> Of Camball and of Algarsife ,
> And who had Canacee to wife,
> That own'd the vertuous ring and glass,
> And of the wondrous hors of brass
> On which the Tartar King did ride."

It was a pious wish, but in speaking of the story as
"half told," Milton used a poet's license. It was hardly
begun!

Whence did Chaucer obtain the materials for this
story so unlike anything else he wrote? It is possible
to guess, though this is all. Prof. Brandl has pointed
out (*Engl. Studien*, xii. 163) that in 1385-86 Leo VI.,
the last King of Armenia (he died an exile in Paris in
1303), was staying in London. It is possible that it
was from one of his followers that Chaucer obtained
his Eastern lore. Armenia was favourably situated for
the development of such a story. It had suffered many
things at the hands of Greeks and Mongols, Turks and
Persians. Armenian writers took the later Greek and
Byzantine authors as their models; Greek romances

would be familiar to them, and they could not be
ignorant of the stories of magic that abounded in Persia
and the East. The names in the Squire's Tale are in
keeping with such a mixed origin. Canacee is the
Greek Κανάκη, Theodera the Greek Θεόδωρα. On the
other hand, Cambiuscan himself is the famous Chingis
(or Genghis) Khan. the title assumed by the great
Mongol prince, Temujin; while Cambalo has its origin
in Kambala, the name of one of his descendants. As
for the names Algarsyf and Elpheta no one, as far as
I know, has yet suggested an origin for them, but they
are certainly not Greek, and do not appear to be
Mongol. One other point may be noted. In ll. 663
64 Chaucer writes:

> "And after wol I speke of Algarsyf,
> How that he wan Theodera to his wif."

This is the only mention of Theodera, and without
pressing the point unduly, it may certainly be said that
she is introduced as if the readers or hearers of the
story would know who she was. If we suppose Chaucer
to be retelling in his own way a story or stories which
others beside himself might have heard at the English
court, the familiarity of this reference would be explained.

In our inability to discover the direct original (or
originals) from which Chaucer borrowed, we have to
fall back on the fact that no old story is really unique.
There is always something else like it, and by the aid
of such "analogues" we may at least learn the kind of
materials for such a tale which were in existence in
Chaucer's day.

(i.) To take first the historical setting of the story,

we must remember that the careers of the great Tartar conquerors of the thirteenth century, and the habits of their people, were well known in Chaucer's day. Ambassadors, mostly Franciscan friars, from the Pope and the King of France, had visited the Tartar Courts, and like modern travellers on their return had written of what they saw and heard. Thus there is the *Historia Mongolorum* of the Franciscan Carpini who went an embassy to Tartary in 1245, and whose narrative (with that of the Dominican Simon de St. Quentin who visited a Tartar general in Persia) was freely used by Vincent de Beauvais (d. 1264) in his *Speculum Historiale*, or "Mirror of History," one of the best known of medieval compilations. In 1253-54 there was another Franciscan ambassador, William de Rubruquis, and later in the century Friar Ricold of Monte Croce, and the two expeditions of the brothers Nicolo and Maffeo Polo. On the second of these (1271-95) Nicolo took with him his son, Marco Polo (d. 1324), whose account of their travels and of the Court of Kublai Kaan is one of the famous books of the world. To these we must add the *Liber de Tartaris* of Hayton, an Armenian prince who died at Poitiers 'in 1308, and the travels of the Franciscan Odoric of Pordenone (d. 1331). From the works of the last two of these, and various other books, that first of arm-chair travellers, the ingenious compiler who wrote under the name of Sir John Mandeville, made up the *Travels* which in Chaucer's day were accessible both in French and Latin, and perhaps in English also. Most of these authors naturally dwell on the enlightened monarch, Kublai Kaan, who ruled at Cambaluc (Kaanbaligh = the city of the Kaan, the modern Pekin) during the second half of the thirteenth century, but they tell also of the founder of the Mongol empire, the ferocious Temujin (1162-1227), who in 1206 took the name Chingis, or Genghis Khan (very mighty ruler), which through the forms Canjus- or Camiuscan (the latter being used by Friar Ricold) becomes Chaucer's Cambyus- or Cambynscan,[1] and Milton's Cambúscan. In almost any of them also may be found an account of the Kaan's birthday feast, and allusions to the strange foods eaten by the Tartars, the two distinctive bits of local colour in the Squire's Tale, as contrasted with the other details about the king and his court which have nothing individual about them. Dr. Skeat, however, like Mr. Keightley before him, finding that these two points are mentioned by Marco Polo, has argued that therefore Marco Polo must have been Chaucer's authority for them. Starting from this theory he has quoted a number of parallel passages in which the coincidences seem no stronger than would naturally arise in two favourable descriptions of a medieval prince, and has rather unkindly suggested that when Chaucer speaks of Sarray he is really thinking of Cambaluc, when he describes Genghis Khan he is thinking of his grandson Kublai, and that, though Kambala was the name of a Tartar prince, the Cambalo, or Cambalus, in the Squire's Tale is taken from the name of the city Cambaluc floating in Chaucer's brain.

---

[1] This derivation of Cambuscan from Chinghiz Khan was first pointed out by Sir Henry Yule in his edition of Marco Polo. In the Harleian and five others of the MSS. of the Canterbury Tales the form used is Cambynscan, but in the Ellesmere MS., now generally adopted as a text, it is said more to resemble Cambyuscan, and as this is in itself more correct, and has been popularized by Milton's (wrongly accented) Cambúscan, it is here adopted.

A very able paper, by Prof. J. M. Manley,[1] demonstrates the needlessness of Prof. Skeat's theory, which has introduced fresh complications into an already complicated story. My own belief is that, though we may illustrate the Squire's Tale from these old accounts of Tartary, and especially from Marco Polo, because he has been so well edited by Colonel Yule, there is very little probability that Chaucer consulted any of them.[2] It is much more likely that he found these details where he found more important parts of his story, *i.e.* in some lost romance. But if we must suppose that he provided his own local colour, we have no right to pin him down to using Marco Polo to the exclusion of other easily accessible authorities.

(ii.) The description of the horse of brass is an important feature in the fragment of the Squire's Tale which we possess, and we are told that it was by aid of the wonderful beast that the Kaan's[3] son, Algarsyf, won his bride Theodera. For a similar story to this we need go no farther than the tale of the Ebony Horse in the *Arabian Nights*, which may be briefly summarized.

At the feast of the Nevrouz, or new day, which is the first of the year and of spring, strangers came to the Persian Court to show their inventions, and receive

---

[1] Publications of the Modern Language Association of America, vol. xi., No. 3.

[2] There are some features in these narratives, *e.g.* the account of the gorgeous dresses worn at the Kaan's feast, which Chaucer with his love of colour could hardly have helped reproducing if he had known them.

[3] It should, perhaps, be stated that it is said to be correct to adopt the spelling Kaan for the emperor, the minor chiefs being called Khans.

rewards for them. One year three sages appear, the first of whom brings a golden peacock which marks the time by flapping its wings; the second a golden man who blows a trumpet at the approach of enemies; the third a sculptured horse, saddled and bridled, by which he can transport himself where he will through the air. Each sage asks the hand of one of the king's daughters, and the owner of the horse being ugly, the third princess objects. At his father's request the king's son examines the horse. He mounts it, turns the peg in its neck, and is carried away before he has learnt the secret how to control the beast he has set in motion. After a long journey he finds a smaller peg in the horse's ear, and the animal descends to earth near the palace of a princess, the daughter of the King of Yemen. The prince makes her acquaintance. He is surprised by her father, offers to fight his whole army, confronts it, and then flies away on the magic horse. Returning, he carries off the princess to his home, but leaves her a little distance off that he may warn his parents of her approach. Then the third sage, the owner of the horse, finds her and carries her off. After some adventures the princess falls into the hands of another king, and to escape his attentions feigns madness. The prince disguises himself as a physician, offers to cure her, and is brought into her presence with this object. The lovers then mount the magic horse together and make their escape.

Now, though the *Arabian Nights* were not known in Europe in Chaucer's day as a collection, this particular story had reached France a century before he wrote, and forms the plot of the romance of Cléomadès, written about 1285, by Adenès le Roi, a minstrel of Brabant,

who may have learnt it from Blanche of France, widow
of the Spanish Infante.   The romance may be summarized as follows :
    Cléomadès is the son of Ynabele, daughter of the
King of Spain, and of Marcadigas, a Sardinian prince.
One day three kings arrive at Seville, while Marcadigas
is celebrating his birthday feast, bringing gifts with
which to woo his three daughters. Melocandis, King
of Barbary, offers a man of gold who blows a trumpet
whenever treason is near.   Baldigano, of Morocco, offers
a golden hen and three chickens which run about and
clap their wings ; while the hideous Crumpart, King of
Bugia (in North Africa), brings a large horse of ebony
which will carry its rider fifty leagues through the air
in an hour.   A long account of Virgil and his skill in
magic (cf. Squire's Tale, l. 231 and note) follows the
description of these gifts.   The other daughters of
Marcadigas are content with their suitors, but the
youngest, Maxima, implores her brother, Cléomadès, to
protect her from King Crumpart.   Cléomadès de-
preciates the horse, and is bidden by Crumpart to try
it.   He mounts without knowing the secret of how to
stop it, and is instantly carried away through the air.
At last he finds the second peg, alights on the roof of a
lofty tower, and entering the house sees a lovely maiden
with whom he falls in love.   Her father, Carmant, King
of Tuscany, seeks to kill him, but he escapes on his
horse, speedily returns, and carries the princess to
Seville.   He thinks it necessary to warn his parents of
her arrival, and in his absence the wicked Crumpart
persuades the princess to mount the horse, jumps up
behind her, and carries her off.   They alight at Salermo,
and are seized by its King, Meniadus.   Crumpart dies, the

princess feigns madness, and Cléomadès rescues her
as in the *Arabian Nights*.[1]

These rough summaries should make it equally
evident that Chaucer did not work directly from these
particular versions, and that he did work from some
other version of the same story. As for Chaucer's horse
being of brass and not of ebony, a steed of brass occurs
in the story of the Third Kalendar in the *Arabian
Nights*; men of brass in the romance of Huon of
Bordeaux beat iron flails before a giant's gateway so
that none may enter, and the famous talking head of
Friar Bacon was also, according to the legend, of
brass.

As for the magic mirror, Mr. Clouston, to whose
essay on the "Magical Elements in the Squire's Tale"
(Chaucer Society, 1888) I must continue to be indebted,
reminds us that the Cup of Zamshid, a legendary Persian
king, enabled its owner to observe all that was passing
in the world; in the Romance of Reynard the Fox, a
mirror of more limited reflection, "of suche vertu that
men myght see therein all that was don within a myle,"
is among the treasures in Reynard's pretended hoard,
and Gower in his *Confessio Amantis* writes:

> Whan Romĕ stood in noble plight
> Virgile, which was tho parfight,
> A mirrour made, of his clergye,
> And sette it in the tounĕs yĕ,
> Of marbre on a piller withoute,
> That they, by thritty mile aboute,

[1] In a third version, a Turkish story, which, in some editions
of the *Arabian Nights*, takes the place of that first quoted, instead
of three sages there is only a single inventor, an Indian, who brings
the magic horse, and plays the same part as Crumpart and the
third sage.

> By day and eke also by nighte,
> In that mirroure beholdé mighte
> Here enemies, if eny were,
> With all here ordenauncé there
> Which they ayein the citee caste.

* *Tho*, then ; *parfight*, perfect ; *clergye*, magic skill ; *yë*, eye ; *marbre*, marble ; *here*, their ; *ayein*, against.

To illustrate the virtues of the magic ring Mr. Clouston has collected numerous stories of rings which conferred on their owners power over demons and genii, as was the case with Solomon's (cp. note to l. 131), immunity from poison, invisibility, the power of gaining love, or boundless wealth. But the only ring with this exact property of rendering the language of birds intelligible is one mentioned in a German story[1] in which

"A prince comes to a castle where all the people are fast asleep (enchanted ?) ; and in a hall of the castle he finds a table on which lay a golden ring, and this inscription was on the table : 'Whosoever puts this ring in his mouth shall understand the language of birds.' He afterwards puts the ring in his mouth, and by understanding what three crows are saying one to another is saved from death.'"

Incidents involving the power of understanding or conversing with beasts and birds are, of course, common in fairy tales, especially in those of Eastern origin.

As to the magic sword, Mr. Clouston has the following note :

"Telephus, the son of Hercules and Auge, was wounded by Achilles with his spear, and healed by the application of the same weapon. Petronius, in his epigram, *De Telepho*, exactly describes the qualities of Cambyuskan's magic sword—

Unde datum est vulnus, contigit inde salus.[2]

---

[1] From Wolff's *Deutsche Hausmarchen*, quoted by Mr. J. G. Frazer in a paper on "The Language of Animals" in the *Archæological Review*, i. 163.

[2] Thence, whence the wound was given, healing comes.

"A somewhat similar sword was possessed by a giant in a Norse tale—'whoever is touched with its point dies instantly; but if he is touched with the hilt he immediately returns to life' (Thorpe's *Yule-Tide Stories*, 1853, p. 162). And in another Norse tale (Dasent's *Tales from the Fjords*) a witch gives the hero a sword, one edge of which was black, the other white. If he smote a foe with the black edge he fell dead in a moment, but by striking him with the white edge the dead man as quickly rose up alive."

These parallels, which the industry of Mr. Clouston has collected, show that the magic gifts which Chaucer introduces in the Squire's Tale were part of the common property of Eastern story-tellers, while the stories of the magic horse show how the most important of them was used by other romancers. But, whereas in other versions the use of the other gifts is merely perfunctory (confined in fact to the golden man blowing his horn when the prince mounts the horse without fully knowing its secret), in Chaucer the ring seems meant to be as important as the horse itself, and as he introduces four gifts instead of three, he probably intended to bring the third and fourth into play as well as the first two. He also adds, as we have seen, other developments, so that the tale, if it had ever been completed, must have been immensely complicated. It is certain that Chaucer must have had at least one earlier story from which to work. It seems highly probable that he had more than one, and that he tried to combine them on too ambitious a scale. So far as the fragment goes it is written in his best and easiest style, and this with the "note of time" in l. 73,[1] in which the narrator shows his anxiety not to take up more than his fair share of

---

[1] Prime (see the Shipman's Tale, ll. 1395-96) was the usual dinner hour, so "I wol not taryen you, for it is pryme" may have had a very special meaning.

the pilgrim's time, proves that the tale was written somewhere about 1388, when the scheme of the *Canterbury Tales* was already well started, and Chaucer's powers were at their highest.

It only remains to add that two attempts have been made to complete this "half-told" tale. The first of these is contained in Canto ii., st. 30—end of Canto iii. of Book iv. of Spenser's *Faery Queene* (published in 1596). Here, not very happily, Spenser makes three brothers, Priamond, Dyamond, and Triamond, "borne at one burden in one happie morne" of the fay Agape, fight with Cambalo to gain the hand of Canacee. Canacee lends Cambalo her ring,

> "That 'mongst the manie vertues which we reed,
> Had power to staunch al wounds that mortally did bleed,"

an extension of the virtues attributed to the ring by Chaucer (ll. 153-55), to which Spenser had access through Lydgate. By the help of the ring Cambalo kills Priamond and Dyamond, but is reconciled to Triamond by the mediation of their sister Cambina, whom he marries.

The second continuation was written by a very minor poet, a certain John Lane, about 1616, and revised by him in 1630. Both versions exist in manuscript, and that of 1616, with the later variations shown as footnotes, was printed in 1888 by the Chaucer Society. Lane introduces all Chaucer's characters, and carries out his complicated plot in all its ramifications, though not always according to the plan which Chaucer sketched out. We need not follow out these differences, for the poem is very poor stuff, and it is almost a pity it has been preserved to demand notice. But Lane was a friend of Milton's father, and it is possible that it may

have been due to this friendship that Milton inserted
in *Il Penseroso* the reference to Chaucer already quoted.
A still nobler reference (not seriously marred by the
mistake which treats the conclusion to the Squire's Tale
as having been written and lost) preludes Spenser's
continuation, and to quote it will give a pleasant ending
to this Introduction.

> "Whylome, as antique stories tellen us,
>   Those two[1] were foes the fellonest on ground,
>   And battell made the dreddest daungerous
>   That ever shrilling trumpet did resound;
>   Though now their acts be nowhere to be found,
>   As that renowmed Poet them compyled
>   With warlike numbers and Heroicke sound, ·
>   Dan Chaucer, well of English undefyled,
>   On Fames eternall beadroll worthie to be fyled.

> "But wicked Time, that all good thoughts doth waste,
>   And workes of noblest wits to nought outweare,
>   That famous moniment hath quite defaste,
>   And robd the world of threasure endlesse deare,
>   The whiche mote have enriched all us heare.
>   O cursed Eld! the cankerworme of writs,
>   How may these rimes, so rude as doth appeare,
>   Hope to endure, sith workes of heavenly wits
>   Are quite devourd, and brought to nought by little bits?

> "Then pardon, O most sacred happie spirit!
>   That I thy labours lost may thus revive,
>   And steale from thee the meede of thy due merit,
>   That none durst ever whilest thou wast alive,
>   And being dead in vaine yet many strive:
>   Ne dare I like; but, through infusion sweete
>   Of thine owne spirit which doth in me survive,
>   I follow here the footing of thy feete,
>   That with thy meaning so I may the rather meete."
>
>   (*F.Q.* IV. 2. xxxii.-xxxiv.)

---

[1] "Couragious Cambell and stout Triamond."

NOTE.—The text of this edition is taken from the Ellesmere Manuscript (E.), collated with the Harleian (H.), Cambridge (C.), Hengwrt (Heng.), Corpus (Corp.), Petworth (P.), and Lansdowne (L.), all as printed by the Chaucer Society. The reading of the Ellesmere manuscript is departed from in the following cases, of which those marked with an asterisk are the more important.

16.*	longed, E.C. longeth.	298.	yow, E.C. me.
17.	as, E. and.	217.	telle yow, E.C. and Heng.
61.*	solempne, E.P. so sol-		yow telle.
	empne.	322.	ther-in, E.C. ther.
62.	ne, E.H. om.	324.*	abyde, E.C. stonde.
86.	spoke, E.C. spoken.	326.	ne, E. and Heng. nor.
96.	come, E.C. comen.	338.	ful ... doughty, E.C. ful,
99.	seyde, E.C. seith.		omitting doughty.
110.	Arabie, E. and Heng.	351.	seyde that it, E.C. seyde
	Arabe.		it.
123.	whan, E. whan that.	377.	is, E. om.
138.	on, E. in.	416.	as, E.C. om.
144.	to, E.C. unto.	421.	he, E.P. she.
158.	kerve, E. hym kerve.	436.	answere, E. answeren.
160.	the stroke, E. a stroke.	449.	this, E. the.
162.	thilke, E.C. that.	455.*	ire, E.C. love.
165.	stroke, E.C. strike.	463.	compassioun, E. passioun.
173.	to, E. unto.	469.	grete, E. the grete.
178.	the, E.C. this.	472.	yet moore, E.C. moore
184.	or, E. ne.		yet.
200.	goon, E. go.	484	that, E. om.
201.	of fairye, E. and Heng. a	487.	set, E.C. y-set.
	fairye, C. as fayre.	489.	to, E. om.
201.	the peple, E.C. al the	491.	chastysed, E. and Heng.
	peple.		chasted.
207.	seyden it, E. seyde that it.	499.	ther, F.C. that.
217.	for it, E. it.	510.*	no wight, E.C. I ne; C. I
226.*	maistre, E.C. hye.		not with a word scratched
232.	speke, E.C. speken.		out.
239.*	for, E.C. with.	520.	this, E. the.
262.	his, E. and Heng. the.	535.	in change of, E. in change
275.	up on, E.C. up in.		for.
288.	over, E.C. of.	548.	Jason, E.C. Troilus.

555. **unbokele**, E. unbokelen.
562. **so**, E.C. *om.*
583. **he**, E. I.
597. **seyde**, E.C. seyde hym.
[1]601.* **wel seyd**, E.C. *om* wel.
623. **and humble**, E. and Pet. humble.

626. **go**, E. and Heng. ago.
639. **salves**, E. and Heng. saves.
647. **were peynted**, E. ther were y-peynted.

[1] *N.B.*—MS. Harley stops at l. 616.

The readings *as stille as* for *stille as* in l. 174, the second *this* in l. 266, the second *the* in l. 291, *wondred* (for *wondreden, wondren*) in l. 307, the *by* in l. 330, and the reading *seme* for *to seme* in l. 394 have the authority of the Harleian MS. only.

Other Harleian readings worth considering, but not adopted in the text, are : omission of *ther* in l. 203; of *hir* in l. 368, of *she* in l. 370, of *more* in l. 429, of *for* in l. 492, and of *propre* in l. 610, also *slake* for *awake* in l. 476.

The reading *thurghout* for *thurgh* in l. 46, and the *and* before *fresh* in l. 622 are supported by the Hengwrt MS. only.

Nas nevere yet no man in l. 423 is supported by Harley and Corpus against *nas nevere man yet*, and *nas nevere yit man* of the other five MSS. ; *al* before *my thoght* in l. 533, by Harley, Cambridge, and Lansdowne against the other four MSS.

See also notes on lines 20, 105, 114, 171, 239, 419, 515, and 602.

A. W. P.

THE CANTERBURY TALES

SQUIRE'S TALE

[*Words of the Host to the Squire*]

'SQUIER, come neer, if it your willé be,
And sey somwhat of love; for certés ye
Konnen theron as muche as any man.'
'Nay, sire,' quod he, 'but I wol seye as I kan
With hertly wyl,—for I wol nat rebelle   5
Agayn youre lust. A talé wol I telle.
Have me excuséd, if I speke amys;
My wyl is good, and lo, my tale is this.'

Here bigynneth the Squieres Tale

AT Sarray, in the land of Tartarye,
Ther dwelte a kyng that werreyéd Russye,   10
Thurgh which ther dydé many a doughty man.
This noble kyng was clepéd Cambyuskan,
Which in his tyme was of so greet renoun
That ther was nowher in no regioun
So excellent a lord in allé thyng.   15

Ⅽ   A

Hym lakkéd noght that longed to a kyng;
As of the secte of which that he was born
He keptc his lay, to which that he was sworn;
And therto he was hardy, wys, and riche,
Pitous and just, and evermore yliche;   20
Sooth of his word, benigne and honurable,
Of his coráge as any centre stable;
Yong, fressh, and strong, in armés desirous
As any bacheler of al his hous.
A fair persone he was, and fortunat,   25
And kepte alwey so wel roial estat
That ther was nowher swich another man.
      This noble kyng, this Tartre Cambyuskan,
Haddé two sones on Elpheta his wyf,
Of whiché the eldeste highté Algarsyf;   30
That oother sone was clepéd Cambalo.
A doghter hadde this worthy kyng also.
That yongest was, and highté Canacee,
But for to tellé yow al hir beautee
It lyth nat in my tonge, nyn my konnyng;   35
I dar nat undertake so heigh a thyng;
Myn Englissh eek is insufficient;
It mosté been a rethor excellent,
That koude his colours longynge for that art,
If he sholde hire discryven every part;   40
I am noon swich, I moot speke as I kan,
      And so bifel that whan this Cambyuskan
Hath twenty wynter born his diademe,
As he was wont fro yeer to yeer, I deme,
He leet the feeste of his nativitee   45

Doon cryen thurghout Sarray his citee,
The last Idus of March after the yeer.
  Phebus, the sonne, ful joly was and cleer,
For he was neigh his exaltacioun
In Martes face, and in his mansioun   50
In Aries, the colerik hoote signe.
Ful lusty was the weder and benigne,
For which the foweles agayn the sonne sheene,
What for the sesoun and the yonge grene,
Ful loude songen hire affecciouns,   55
Hem semed han geten hem protecciouns
Agayn the swerd of wynter, keene and coold.
  This Cambyuskan—of which I have yow toold—
In roial vestiment sit on his deys,
With diademe, ful heighe in his paleys,   60
And halt his feeste solempne and so ryche,
That in this world ne was ther noon it lyche;
Of which, if I shal tellen al tharray,
Thanne wolde it occupie a someres day;
And eek it nedeth nat for to devyse   65
At every cours the ordre of hire servyse.
I wol nat tellen of hir strange sewes, *clia in*
Ne of hir swannes, ne of hire heronsewes.
Eek in that lond, as tellen knyghtes olde,
Ther is som mete that is ful deynte holde   70
That in this lond men recche of it but smal;
Ther nys no man that may reporten al.
  I wol nat taryen yow, for it is pryme,
And for it is no fruyt, but los of tyme;
Unto my firste I wole have my recours.   75

And so bifel that after the thriddė cours,
Whil that this kyng sit thus in his noblėyc,
Herknynge his mynstralės hir thyngės pleye
Biforn hym at the bord deliciously,
In at the hallė dore, al sodeynly,   80
Ther cam a knyght upon a steedc of bras,
And in his hand a brood mirour of glas;
Upon his thombe he haddc of gold a ring,
And by his syde a naked swerd hangyng;
And up he rideth to the hcighė bord.   85
In al the hallė ne was ther spoke a word,
For merveille of this knyght; hym to biholdc
Ful bisily ther wayten yonge and olde.
 This strangė knyght that cam thus sodeynly,
Al armėd, save his heed, ful richėly,   90
Saleweth kyng and queene, and lordės alle,
By ordre, as they seten in the halle,
With so heigh reverence and obeisaunce,
As wel in spechė as in contenaunce,
That Gawayn, with his oldė curteisye,   95
Though he were come ageyn out of fairyc,
Ne koude hym nat amendė with a word;
And after this, biforn the heighė bord,
He with a manly voys seyde his message
After the forme usėd in his langagc,   100
Withouten vice of silable, or of lettre;
And for his talė sholdė seme the bettre,
Accordant to his wordės was his cheere,
As techeth art of speche hem that it leere.
Al be that I kan nat sowne his stile,   105

Ne kan nat clymben over so heigh a style,
Yet seye I this, as to commune entente,
Thus muche amounteth al that ever he mente,
If it so be that I have it in mynde.
He seyde, 'The kyng of Arabie and of Inde, 110
My ligé lord, on this solempné day
Saleweth yow, as he best kan and may,
And sendeth yow, in honour of youre feeste,
By me, that am al redy at youre heeste,
This steede of bras, that esily and weel   115
Kan in the space of o day natureel,—
This is to seyn, in foure and twenty houres,—
Wher so yow lyst, in droghte or ellés shoures,
Beren youre body into every place
To which youre herté wilneth for to pace,   120
Withouten wem of yow, thurgh foul or fair ;
Or, if yow lyst to fleen as hye in the air
As dooth an egle whan hym list to soore,
This samé steede shal bere yow ever moore,
Withouten harm, til ye be ther yow leste,   125
Though that ye slepen on his bak, or reste ;
And turne ageyn with writhyng of a pyn.
He that it wroghté koude ful many a gyn.
He wayted many a constellacioun
Er he had doon this operacioun,   130
And knew ful many a seel, and many a bond.
2.   'This mirrour eek, that I have in myn hond,
Hath swich a myght that men may in it see
Whan ther shal fallen any adversitee
Unto youre regne, or to youreself also,   135

And openly who is youre freend or foo;
And over al this, if any lady bright
Hath set hire herte on any maner wight,
If he be fals she shal his tresoun see,
His newe love, and al his subtiltee,   140
So openly that ther shal no thyng hyde.
Wherfore, ageyn this lusty someres tyde,
This mirour and this ryng that ye may see
He hath sent to my lady Canacee,
Youre excellente doghter that is heere.   145
     'The vertu of the ryng, if ye wol heere,
Is this, that if hire lust it for to were
Upon hir thombe, or in hir purs it bere,
Ther is no fowel that fleeth under the hevene
That she ne shal wel understonde his stevene,   150
And knowe his menyng openly and pleyn,
And answere hym in his langage ageyn;
And every gras that groweth upon roote
She shal eek knowe and whom it wol do boote,
Al be his woundes never so depe and wyde.   155
     'This naked swerd that hangeth by my syde
Swich vertu hath that what man so ye smyte,
Thurghout his armure it wol kerve and byte,
Were it as thikke as is a branched ook;
And what man that is wounded with the strook
Shal never be hool, til that yow list of grace   161
To stroke hym with the plat in thilke place
Ther he is hurt; this is as muche to seyn, .
Ye moote with the platte swerd ageyn
Stroke hym in the wounde and it wol close.   165

This is a verray sooth, withouten glose,
It failleth nat whil it is in youre hoold.'
And whan this knyght hath thus his talé toold,
He rideth out of halle, and doun he lighte.
His steedé, which that shoon as sonné brighte,   170
Stant in the court as stille as any stoon.
This knyght is to his chambré lad anoon,
And is unarméd and to mete y-set.
The presentes been ful roially y-fet,—
This is to seyn, the swerd and the mirour,—   175
And born anon into the heighé tour,
With certeine officers ordeyned therfore ;
And unto Canacee the ryng was bore
Solempnély, ther she sit at the table ;
But sikerly, withouten any fable,   180
The hors of bras, that may nat be remewed,
It stant as it were to the ground y-glewed ;
Ther may no man out of the place it dryve
For noon engyn of wyndas or polyve ;
And causé why ? for they kan nat the craft ;   185
And therfore in the place they han it laft,
Til that the knyght hath taught hem the manere
To voyden hym, as ye shal after heere.
    Greet was the prees that swarmeth to and fro
To gauren on this hors that stondeth so ;   190
For it so heigh was, and so brood and long,
So wel proporcioned for to been strong,
Right as it were a steede of Lumbardye ;
Ther-with so horsly, and so quyk of eye,
As it a gentil Poilleys courser were ;   195

For certés, fro his tayl unto his ere,
Nature ne art ne koude hym nat amende
In no degree, as al the peple wende.
But evermoore hir mooste wonder was
How that it koude goon, and was of bras!   200
It was of fairye, as the peple semed.
Diversé folk diversely they demed;
As many heddes as. manye wittes ther been.
They murmureden as dooth a swarm of been,
And maden skiles after hir fantasies,   205
Rehersynge of thise oldé poetries;
And seyden it was lyk the Pegasee,
The hors that haddé wyngés for to flee
Or elles it was the Grekés hors, Synoun,
That broghté Troié to destruccioun,   210
As men may in thise oldé geestés rede.
    'Myn herte.' quod oon, 'is evermoore in drede;
I trowe.som men of armés been ther-inne,
That shapen hem this citee for to wynne;
It were right good that al swich thyng were knowe.'
    Another rownéd to his felawe lowe,   216
And seyde, 'He lyeth! for it is rather lyk
An apparence, y-maad by som magyk;
As jogelours pleyen at thise feestés grete.'
Of sondry doutés thus they jangle and trete,   220
As lewéd peple demeth comunly
Of thyngés that been maad moore subtilly
Than they kan in hir lewednesse comprehende,
They demen gladly to the badder ende.
    And somme of hem wondred on the mirour   225

That born was up into the maistre tour,
How men myghte in it swiché thyngés se.
Another answerde and seyde it myghte wel be
Naturelly, by composiciouns
Of angles, and of slye reflexiouns;   230
And seyden that in Romé was swich oon.
They speke of Alocen and Vitulon,
And Aristotle, that writen in hir lyves
Of queynté mirours, and of prospectives,
As knowen they that han hir bookés herd.   235
    And oother folk ,han wondred on the swerd
That woldé percen thurghout every thyng;
And fille in speche of Thelóphus the kyng,
And of Achilles for his queynté spere,
For he koude with it bothé heele and dere,   240
Right in swich wise as men may with the swerd
Of which right now ye han youre-selven herd.
They speken of sondry hardyng of metal,
And speke of medicynés therwithal,
And how and whanne it sholde y-harded be,   245
Which is unknowe, algatés unto me.
    Tho speeké they of Canacëes ryng,
And seyden alle that swich a wonder thyng
Of craft of ryngés herde they never noon;
Save that he Moyses and kyng Salomon   250
Hadden a name of konnyng in swich art;
Thus seyn the peple and drawen hem apart.
    But nathélees somme seiden that it was
Wonder to maken of fern-asshen glas,
And yet nys glas nat lyk asshen of fern,   255

But for they han i-knowen it so fern
Therfore cesseth hir janglyng and hir wonder.
   As soore wondren somme on cause of thonder,
On ebbe, on flood, on gossomer, and on myst,
And on alle thyng til that his cause is wyst,   260
Thus jangle they, and demen and devyse,
Til that the kyng gan fro the bord aryse.
   Phebus hath laft the angle meridional,
And yet ascendynge was the beest roial,
The gentil Leon, with his Aldrian,   265
Whan that this Tartre kyng this Cambyuskan
Roos fro his bord, ther as he sat ful hye.
Toforn hym gooth the loude mynstralcye
Til he cam to his chambre of parementz ;
Ther as they sownen diverse instrumentz,   270
That is y-like an hevene for to heere.
Now dauncen lusty Venus children deere,
For in the Fyssh hir lady sat ful hye,
And looketh on hem with a freendly eye.
   This noble kyng is set up on his trone ;   275
This strange knyght is fet to hym ful soone,
And on the daunce he gooth with Canacee.
Heere is the revel and the jolitee
That is nat able a dul man to devyse ;
(He moste han knowen love and his servyse,   280
And been a feestlych man, as fressh as May,
That sholde yow devysen swich array)
   Who koude telle yow the forme of daunces
So unkouthe, and so fresshe contenaunces,
Swich subtil lookyng and dissymulynges   285

For drede of jalouse mennes aperceyvynges?
No man but Launcelet, and he is deed.
Therfore I passe over al this lustiheed ;
I sey namoore, but in this jolynesse
I lete hem til men to the soper dresse.   290
The styward byt the spices for to hye,
And eek the wyn, in al this melodye.
The usshers and the squiers been y-goon,
The spices and the wyn is come anoon. .
They ete and drynke, and whan this hadde an
      ende,   295
Unto the temple, as reson was, they wende.
The service doon they soupen al by day ; '
What nedeth yow rehercen hire array ?
Ćch man woot wel that a kynges feeste
Hath plentee to the mooste and to the leeste, 300
And deyntees mo than been in my knowyng.
   At after soper gooth this noble kyng
To seen this hors of bras, with all the route
Of lordes and of ladyes hym aboute.
Swich wondryng was ther on this hors of bras 305
That syn the grete sege of Troie was,—
Ther as men wondred on an hors also,—
Ne was ther swich a wondryng as was tho. ·
But fynally, the kyng axeth this knyght
The vertu of this courser, and the myght,   310
And preyede hym to telle his governaunce.
   This hors anoon bigan to trippe and daunce
Whan that this knyght leyde hand upon his reyne,
And seyde, 'Sire, ther is namoore to seyne,

But whan yow list to ryden anywhere   315
Ye mooten trille a pyn, stant in his ere,
Which I shal tellé yow bitwix us two.
Ye móoté nempne hym to what place also,
Or to what contree, that yow list to ryde;
And whan ye come ther as yow list abyde,   320
Bidde hym descende, and trille another pyn,—
For therin lith theffect of al the gyn,—
And he wol doun descende and doon youre wille,
And in that place he wol abidé stille.
Though al the world the contrarie hadde y-swore,
He shal nat thennés been y-drawe ne y-bore;   326
Or, if yow listé bidde hym thennés goon,
Trillé this pyn, and he wol vanysshe anoon
Out of the sighte of every maner wight,
And come agayn, be it by day or nyght,   330
Whan that yow list to clepen hym ageyn
In swich a gyse as I shal to yow seyn,
Bitwixé yow and me, and that ful soone.
Ride whan yow list, ther is namoore to doone.'

    Enforméd whan the kyng was of that knyght,   335
And hath conceyvéd in his wit aright
The manere and the forme of al this thyng,
Ful glad and blithe this noble doughty kyng
Repeireth to his revel as biforn.

    The brydel is unto the tour y-born   340
And kept among his jueles leeve and deere,
The hors vanysshed, I noot in what manere,
Out of hir sighte,—ye gete namoore of me;
But thus I lete in lust and jolitee

This Cambyuskan his lordés festeiynge,   345
Til wel ny the day bigan to sprynge.

[PART II]

The norice of digestioun, the sleepe,
Gan on hem wynke, and bad hem taken keepe
That muchel drynke and labour wolde han reste;
And with a galpyng mouth hem alle he keste,   350
And seyde, that it was tyme to lye adoun,
For blood was in his domynacioun.
'Cherisseth blood, natúrés freend,' quod he.
They thanken hym galpynge, by two, by thre,
And every wight gan drawe hym to his reste,   355
As sleepe hem bad; they tooke it for the beste.

Hire dremés shul nat been y-toold for me;
Ful were hire heddés of fumositee,
That causeth dreem, of which ther nys no charge.
They slepen til that it was prymé large,   360
The moosté part, but it were Canacee.
She was ful mesuráble, as wommen be;.
For of hir fader hadde she také leve
To goon to reste, soone after it was eve.
Hir listé nat appalléd for to be,   365
Ne on the morwe unfeestlich for to se,
And slepte hire firsté sleepe and thanne awook;
For swich a joyé she in hir herté took,
Bothe of hir queynté ryng and hire mirour,
That twenty tyme she changéd hir colour,   370
And in hire sleepe, right for impressioun

Of hire mirour, she hadde a visioun.
Wherfore er that the sonné gan up glyde
She clepéd on hir maistresse hire bisyde,
And seydé that hire listé for to ryse. 375
Thise oldé wommen that ·been gladly wyse,
As is hire maistresse, answerde hire anon,
And seydé, 'Madame, whider wil ye goon
Thus erly, for the folk been alle on reste?'
'I wol,' quod she, 'arisé,—for me leste 380
No lenger for to slepe,—and walke aboute.'
Hire maistresse clepeth wommen a greet route,
And up they rysen, wel a ten or twelve;
Up riseth fresshé Canacee hir-selve,
As rody and bright as dooth the yongé sonne 385
That in the Ram is foure degrees up ronne.
Noon hyer was he whan she redy was,
And forth she walketh esily a´pas,
Arrayed after the lusty sesoun soote
Líghtly, for to pleye and walke on foote, 390
Nat but with fyve or sixe of hir meynee,
And in a trench, forth in the park, gooth she.
The vapour, which that fro the erthé glood,
Madé the sonné semé rody and brood,
But nathélees it was so fair a sighte 395
That it made alle hire hertés for to lighte,—
What for the sesoun, and the morwénynge,
And for the foweles that she herdé synge;
For right anon she wisté what they mente
Right by hir song, and knew al hire entente. 400

The knottė why that every tale is toold,
If it be taried til that lust be coold
Of hem that han it after herkned yoore,
The savour passeth ever lenger the moore,
For fulsomnesse of his prolixitee ;   405
And by the samė resoun thynketh me,
I sholdė to the knottė condescende
And maken of hir walkyng soone an ende.
  Amydde a tree fordrye, as whit as chalk,
As Canacee was pleyyng in hir walk,   410
Ther sat a faucon over hire heed ful hye,
That with a pitous voys so gan to crye
That all the wode resounėd of hire cry.
Y-beten hath she hir-self so pitously
With bothe hir wyngės til the redė blood   415
Ran endėlong the tree ther as she stood,
And ever in oon she cryde alwey and shrighte,
And with hir beek hir-selven so she prighte,
That ther nys tygre noon, ne crueel beest,
That dwelleth outher in wode or in forest,   420
That nolde han wept, if that he wepė koude,
For sorwe of hire, she shrighte alwey so loude ;
For ther nas never yet no man on lyve,—
If that I koude a faucon wel discryve,—
That herde of swich another of fairnesse,   425
As wel of plumage as of gentillesse
Of shape, and al that myghte y-rekened be.
A faucon peregryn thanne semėd she
Of fremdė land, and evermoore, as she stood,   429
She swowneth now and now for lakke of blood,

Til wel neigh is she fallen fro the tree.

This fairè kyngès doghter, Canacee,
That on hir fynger baar the queyntè ryng,
Thurgh which she understood wel every thyng
That any fowel may in his ledenè seyn,   435
And koude answere hym in his ledene ageyn,
Hath understondè what this faucon seyde,
And wel neigh for the routhe almoost she deyde;
And to the tree she gooth ful hastily,
And on this faukon looketh pitously,   440
And heeld hir lappe abrood, for wel she wiste
The faukon mostè fallen fro the twiste,
Whan that it swownèd next, for lakke of blood.
A longè while to wayten hire she stood,
Til attè laste she spak in this manere   445
Unto the hauk, as ye shal after heere:
     'What is the cause, if it be for to telle,
That ye be in this furial pyne of helle?'
Quod Canacee unto the hauk above.
'Is this for sorwe of deeth, or los of love?   450
For, as I trowè, thise been causes two
That causen moost a gentil hertè wo.
Of oother harm it nedeth nat to speke,
For ye youre-self upon your-self yow wreke,
Which proveth well that outher ire or drede   455
Moot been enchesoun of youre cruel dede,
Syn that I see noon oother wight yow chace.
For love of God, as dooth youre-selven grace,
Or what may been youre helpe; for West nor Est
Ne saugh I never, er now, no bryd ne beest   460

That ferdé with hymself so pitously.
Ye sle me with youre sorwé, verrailly ;
I have of yow so greet compassioun.
For Goddés love, com fro the tree adoun ;
And, as I am a kyngés doghter trewe,　　　　465
If that I verraily the causé knewe
Of youre disese, if it lay in my myght,
I wolde amenden it er it were nyght,
As wisly helpe me greté God of kyndé !
And herbés shal I right ynowe y-fynde　　　　470
To heelé with youre hurtés hastily.'
　　Tho shrighte this faucon yet moore pitously
Than ever she dide, and fil to grounde anon,
And lith aswowné, deed, and lyk a stoon,
Til Canacee hath in hire lappe hire take　　　　475
Unto the tyme she gan of swough awake ;
And after that she of hir swough abreyde
Right in hir haukés ledene thus she seyde :
'That pitee renneth soone in gentil hertc,
Feelyngc his similitude in peynés smerte,　　　　480
Is prevéd al day, as men may it see,
As wel by werk as by auctoritee ;
For gentil herté kitheth gentillesse.
I se wel that ye han of my distresse
Compassioun, my fairé Canacee,　　　　485
Of verray wommanly benignytee
That nature in youre principles hath set ;
But for noon hopé for to fare the bet,
But for to obeye unto youre herté free,
And for to maken othere be war by me,　　　　490

ıı

As by the whelpe chastysed is the leoun,
Right for that cause and for that conclusioun,
Whil that I have a leýser and a space,
Myn harm I wol confessen, er I pace.'
And ever whil that oon hir sorwé tolde   495
That oother weepe as she to water wolde,
Til that the faucon bad hire to be stille,
And, with a syk, right thus she seyde hir wille.
  'Ther I was bred, allas! that hardé day,—
And fostred in a roche of marbul gray   500
So tendrély that no thyng eyléd me,—
I nysté nat what was adversitee
Til I koude flee ful hye under the sky—
Tho dwelte a tercélét me fasté by,
That seméd welle of allé gentillesse;   505
Al were he ful of tresoun and falsnesse,
It was so wrappéd under humble cheere,
And under hewe of trouthe in swich manere,
Under plesance, and under bisy peyne,
That no wight koude han wend he koudé feyne,
So depe in greyn he dyéd his coloures.   511
Right as a serpent hit hym under floures
Til he may seen his tymé for to byte,
Right so this god of love, this ypocryte,
Dooth so his cerymonyes and obeisaunces,   515
And kepeth in semblant alle his observaunces
That sowneth into gentillesse of love.
As in a toumbe is al the faire above,
And under is the corps, swich as ye woot,
Swich was this ypocrite, bothe coold and hoot,   520

And in this wise he servèd his entente,
That save the feend, noon wistè what he mente
Til he so longe hadde wopen and compleyned,
And many a yeer his service to me feyned,
Til that myn herte, to pitous and to nyce,   525
Al innocent of his corouned malice,
For-ferèd of his deeth, as thoughtè me,
Upon his othès and his seurètee, .
Graunted hym love upon this condicioun,
That evermoore myn honour and renoun   530
Were savèd, bothè privee and apert:
This is to seyn, that after his desert,
I yaf hym al myn herte and al my thoght,—
God woot, and he, that otherwisè noght,—
And took his herte in chaunge of myn for ay;
But sooth is seyd, goon sithen many a day,   536
"A trewe wight and a theef thenken nat oon";
And whan he saugh the thyng so fer y-goon
That I hadde graunted hym fully my love,
In swich a gyse as I have seyd above,   540
And yeven hym my trewè herte as fre
As he swoor he yaf his hertè to me;
Anon this tigre ful of doublenesse
Fil on his knees with so devout humblesse,
With so heigh reverence, and, as by his cheere,
So lyk a gentil lovere of manere,   546
So ravysshed, as it semèd, for the joye,
That never Jason, ne Parys of Troye,—
Jason? Cèrtès, ne noon oother man
Syn Lameth was, that alderfirst bigan   550

To loven two, as writen folk biforn;
Ne never, syn the firstė man was born,
Ne koudė man, by twenty thousand part,
Countrefetė the sophymes of his art,
Ne werė worthy unbokele his galoche   555
Ther doublenesse or feynyng sholde approche,
Ne so koude thanke a wight as he dide me!
His manere was an hevene for to see
Til any womman, were she never so wys,
So peynted he, and kembde at point-devys,   560
As wel his wordės as his contenaunce;
And I so loved hym for his obeisaunce,
And for the trouthe I demėd in his herte,
That if so were that any thyng hym smerte,
Al were it never so lite, and I it wiste,   565
Me thoughte I feltė deeth myn hertė twiste;
And shortly, so ferforth this thyng is went,
That my wyl was his willės instrument,—
This is to seyn, my wyl obeyed his wyl
In allė thyng, as fer as resoun fil,   570
Kepynge the boundės of my worshipe ever;
Ne never hadde I thyng so lief, ne lever,
As hym, God woot! ne never shal namo.
This lasteth lenger than a yeer or two
That I supposėd of hym noght but good;   575
But finally thus attė laste it stood,
That Fortune woldė that he mostė twynne
Out of that plaçė which that I was inne.
Wher me was wo, that is no questioun;
I kan nat make of it discripsioun,   580

For o thyng dare I tellen boldély,
I knowe what is the peyne of deeth ther-by;
Swich harme I felte for he ne myghte bileve!
So on a day of me he took his leve,
So sorwful eek that I wende verraily   585
That he had felt as muché harm as I,
Whan that I herde hym speke and saugh his hewe;
But nathélees I thoughte he was so trewe,
And eek that he repairé sholde ageyn
Withinne a litel whilé, sooth to seyn,   590
And resoun wolde eek that he mosté go
For his honóur, as ofte it happeth so,
That I made vertu of necessitee,—
And took it wel, syn that it mosté be.
As I best myghte I hidde fro hym my sorwe   595
And took hym by the hond, Seint John to borwe,
And seydé thus: "Lo, I am yourés al;
Beth swich as I to yow have been and shal."
What he answerde it nedeth noght reherce;
Who kan sey bet than he, who kan do werse?   600
Whan he hath al wel seyd, thanne hath he doon.
"Therfore bihoveth hire a ful long spoon
That shal ete with a feend," thus herde I seye;
So atté laste he mosté forth his weye,
And forth he fleeth til he cam ther hym leste, 605
Whan it cam hym to purpos for to reste.
I trowe he haddé thilké text in mynde,
That "Allé thyng repeiryngé to his kynde
Gladeth hymself,"—thus seyn men, as I gesse.
Men loven of propré kyndé newefangelnessé,   610

As briddès doon that men in cages fede;
For though thou nyght and day take of hem hede,
And strawe hir cagè faire, and softe as silk,
And yeve hem sugre, hony, breed and milk,
Yet right anon as that his dore is uppe,   615
He with his feet wol spurne adoun his cuppe,
And to the wode he wole, and wormès ete;
So newèfangel been they of hire mete
And loven novelrie of proprè kynde,
No gentillesse of blood [ne] may hem bynde.   620
'So ferde this tercèlet, allas, the day!
Though he were gentil born, and fressh and gay,
And goodlich for to seen, and humble and free.
He saugh upon a tyme a kytè flee,
And sodeynly he loved this kytè so   625
That al his love is clenè fro me go,
And hath his trouthè falsèd in this wyse.
Thus hath the kyte my love in hire servyse,
And I am lorn withouten remedie.'
And with that word this faucon gan to crie,   630
And swownèd eft in Canacèès barm.
   Greet was the sorwè for the haukès harm
That Canacee and alle hir wommen made;
They nystè how they myghte the faucon glade,
But Canacee hom bereth hire in hir 'lappe,   635
And softèly in plastres gan hire wrappe,
Ther as she with hire beek haddè hurt hirselve.
Now kan nat Canacee but herbès delve
Out of the ground, and makè salvès newe
Of herbès preciouse, and fyne of hewe,   640

To heelen with this hauk ; fro day to nyght
She dooth hire bisynesse and al hir myght,
And by hire beddes heed she made a mewe,
And covered it with veluettes blewe,
In signe of trouthe that is in wommen sene,   645
And al withoute the mewe is peynted grene,
In which were peynted alle thise false fowles,
As beth thise tidyves, tercelettes and owles ;
And pyes, on hem for to crie and chyde,
Right for despit, were peynted hem bisyde.   650
    Thus lete I Canacee, hir hauk kepyng,
I wol namoore as now speke of hir ryng
Til it come eft to purpos for to seyn
How that this faucon gat hire love ageyn,
Repentant, as the storie telleth us,   655
By mediacioun of Cambalus,
The kynges sone, of whiche I yow tolde ;
But hennes-forth I wol my proces holde
To speke of aventures and of batailles,
That never yet was herd so greet mervailles.   660
    First wol I telle yow of Cambyuskan,
That in his tyme many a citee wan ;
And after wol I speke of Algarsif,
How that he wan Theodera to his wif,
For whom ful ofte in greet peril he was,   665
Ne hadde he ben holpe by the steede of bras ;
And after wol I speke of Cambalo,
That faught in lystes with the bretheren two
For Canacee, er that he myghte hire wynne ;
And ther I lefte I wol ageyn bigynne.   670

[PART III]

Appollo whirleth up his chaar so hye,
Til that the god Mercurius hous, the slye—

  .   .   .   .

*Heere folwen the wordes of the Frankelyn to the Squier,
and the wordes of the Hoost to the Frankelyn*

'In feith, Squier, thow hast thee wel y-quit
And gentilly, I preisė wel thy wit,'   674
Quod the Frankeleyn, 'considerynge thy yowthe
So feelyngly thou spekest, sire, I allowe the,
As to my doom ther is noon that is heere
Of eloquencė that shal be thy peere,
If that thou lyve! God yevė thee good chaunce,
And in vertu sende thee continuaunce;   680
For of thy speche I havė greet deyntėe.
I have a sone, and, by the Trinitee!
I haddė levere than twenty pound worth lond,
Though it right now were fallen in myn hond,
He were a man of swich discrecioun   685
As that ye been; fy on possessioun,
But if a man be vertuous withal!
I have my sonė snybbėd and yet shal,
For he to vertu listeth nat entende,
But for to pleye at dees, and to despende   690
And lese al that he hath, is his usage;
And he hath levere talken with a page
Than to comune with any gentil wight,
There he myghte lernė gentillesse aright.'   694

'Straw for youre "gentillessé,"' quod our Hoost.
'What! Frankéleyn, *pardee*, sire, wel thou woost
That ech of yow moot tellen atté leste
A tale or two, or breken his biheste.'
'That knowe I wel, sire,' quod the Frankéleyn,
'I prey yow haveth me nat in desdeyn   700
Though to this man I speke a word or two.'
'Telle on thy tale, withouten wordés mo!'
'Gladly, sire Hoost,' quod he, 'I wole obeye
Unto your wyl; now herkneth what I seye.
I wol yow nat contrarien in no wyse   705
As fer as that my wittés wol suffyse;
I prey to God that it may plesen yow,
Thanne woot I wel that it is good ynow.'

NOTES.

1. **Squier.** Three manuscripts omit these eight lines, two others read *Sire Frankeleyn*, and the Harley MS. has *Sir Squier.* But the rhyme of *Squier—bacheler* in the *Prologue* (ll. 79, 80) shows that the word was a dissyllable, accented on the last ; and with this pronunciation there is no room for the *Sire.*

2. **sey somwhat of love,** etc. In the *Prologue* the Squire is described as "a lovyere and a lusty bacheler," and we are told of his "hope to stonden in his lady grace," and of the love that caused him to sleep "namoore than dooth a nyghtyngale."

9. **Sarray, in the land of Tartarye.** According to a note in Col. Yule's *Marco Polo* (vol. i., p. 5), Sarai was a city on the banks of the Akhtuba branch of the Wolga, founded by Bātū Khan, who died in 1257. In the next century it was described as "a very handsome and populous city, so large that it made half a day's journey to ride through it." It was destroyed by Timur on his second invasion of Kipchak (1395-96), and extinguished by the Russians a century later.

10. **that werreyed Russye.** "Russia was overrun with fire and sword as far as Tver and Torshok by Bātū Khan (1237-38), some years before his invasion of Poland and Silesia. Tartar tax-gatherers were established in the Russian cities as far north as Rostrov and Jaroslawl, and for many years Russian princes, as far as Novgorod, paid homage to the Mongol Khans in their court at Sarai" (Yule's *Marco Polo*). It is noteworthy that Chaucer tells us of the Squire's father, the good knight (*Prologue*, 54-55):

> "In Lettow hadde he reysed and in Ruce,—
> No cristen man se ofte of his degree."

These Russian campaigns would be against the Tartars.

12. **Cambyuskan**: see Introduction.

20. **Pitous and just, and evermore yliche**: this with the spelling *pietous* is the reading of the Hengwrt MS. ; the others have *And pitous and just alwey y-liche*, which, as Prof. Skeat points out, can be made to scan by reading *pietous* for *pitous.*

22. **as any centre stable.** For the idea of 'centre' as the "point,

pivot, axis, or line, round which a body turns or revolves," and so an emblem of stability as compared with motion, the *New Eng. Dict.* quotes this passage, and, among others, Milton, *Par. Regained*, iv. 534 :

"As a rock
Of Adamant, and as a centre, firm,"

and Carlyle, *French Revolution*, III. v. v. 197, "Not even an Anarchy, but must have a centre to revolve round."

23. **in armes desirous**, apparently a stock phrase. Of the five quotations in the *New Eng. Dict.* for this use of 'desirous' (= eager), four link the word with 'arms.'

24. **bacheler**, a young knight ; strictly, one "not old enough, or having too few vassals, to display his own banner, and who therefore followed the banner of another" (*N.E.D.*).

25. **fortunat.** Chaucer probably means not merely that Cambyuskan had enjoyed good luck, but that he had been born under what astrologers considered a "lucky star."

29. **Elpheta.** No one has yet proposed any explanation of this name, or of Algarsyf in the next line. They are not the kind of names which Chaucer would invent ; and till they have been traced, we may be quite sure that we have not found the sources which he used for this story.

31. **Cambalo.** Keightley (see Introduction) suggests that this name was taken from that of Cambaluc, Kublai Khan's capital. But Kambala is a Tartar name, and the hypothesis seems unnecessary.

33. **Canacee.** There is a story of a Canacé in Ovid's *Heroides*, Ep. xi., imitated by Gower in his *Confessio Amantis*. But as Chaucer reprobates this story in the prologue to the *Man of Law's Tale* (B 77-79), he would hardly have taken the name for his heroine if it had not occurred in the (unknown) source of this tale.

37. **Myn Englissh eek is insufficient.** For the phrase "Myn Englissh," cp. the description of the Friar (*Prologue*, 264-65) :

"Somewhat he lipsed for his wantownesse,
To make his Englissh sweet upon his tonge."

In the fourteenth century, when English was only just completing its victory over French, the use of the word, where we should now only say 'language,' is significant. Cp. *Legend of Good Women* (Text B), 66, 67 :

"Allas, that I ne had Englyssh, ryme or prose,
Súffisant this flour to preyse aryght ! "

See also *Dethe of Blaunche*, 894-98.

39. **his colours longynge for that art**, ornaments of style that belong to rhetoric. Cp. *Franklin's Prologue* (F 723-25) :

"Colours ne knowe I none, withouten drede,
But swiche colours as growen in the mede,
Or elles swiche as men dye or peynte."

40. hire discryven every part : 'every part' is here used adverbi-
ally, as Chaucer elsewhere uses, with the same meaning, 'everydel.'
Cp. *Dethe of Blaunche*, 231-32 :
> " When I hadde red this tale wel,
> And over-loked hit everydel."

45. the feeste of his nativitee. For these Tartar feasts on the
birthday of their Khan, see *Marco Polo* (Yule's translation), book ii.,
chap. 4: "You must know that the Tartars keep high festival yearly
on their birthdays. ... Now, on his birthday the Great Kaan dresses
in the best of his robes, all wrought with beaten gold, and full
12,000 Barons and Knights on that day come forth dressed in robes
of the same colour. ... On his birthday also, all the Tartars in the
world, and all the countries and governments that owe allegiance to
the Kaan, offer him great presents according to their several ability,
and as prescription or orders have fixed the amount." A similar
feast, also made an occasion for much present giving, was held at
the beginning of the Tartar New Year, in February. This was
called the "White Feast." A similar account, borrowed from
Odoric of Pordenone, is given by Mandeville in his chapter "Of the
Governance of the great Khan's Court."

45-46. leet ... Doon cryen, a pleonasm. Cp. *Merlin*, 57 : " The
kyng dide do make this dragon," the logical subject (men, somebody,
etc.) being in each case omitted.

47. The last Idus of March. The first day of the Roman month
was called the Kalends, the 5th or (as in March) the 7th day the
Nones, the 13th or (as in March) the 15th day the Ides. Days falling between these dates were reckoned from the one next ensuing,
as *e.g.* the 8th, 7th, 6th day before the Ides. The 'last Idus' means
the Ides themselves, *i.e.* March 15th.

    after the yeer, according to the season.

49-51. Phebus ... was neigh his exaltacioun, etc. The sun
entered the sign of Aries, or the Ram, on March 12th (in Chaucer's
day), and reached his exaltation on March 30th. A face is a third,
or ten degrees, of a sign, and the first face in Aries (*i.e.* March 12th
to 21st) was called the face of Mars. The sign of the Ram was the
diurnal house or mansion of Mars, to whom (and not to Phoebus)
the 'his' in l. 50 refers. See Chaucer's *Astrology*, §§ 3 and 5.

51. Aries, the colerik hoote signe. In the *Kalender of Shepherds*,
a fifteenth century almanack, we are told that Aries is one of the
three hot or fiery signs, and that the child born under it shall be
" soon angry and soon appesyd."

53. For which the foweles, etc. Cp. *Prologue*, where, when the
sun has finished his course in Aries, *i.e.* after April 11th, for delight
of the spring "the smale foweles maken melodye." Cp. also the
roundel in the *Parlement of Foules* with its refrain (691-93) :
> " Now welcom, somer, with thy sonne softe,
> Thou hast this wintres weders overshake
> And driven a-wey the longe nyghtes blake."

59. **deys** (*dais*, a raised platform), monosyllabic to rhyme with
'paleys.' The *New Eng. Dict.* notes "the word died out in England about 1600, its recent revival is due to historical and antiquarian
writers. ... Always a monosyllable in French, and in English, where
retained as a living word, the dissyllabic pronunciation is a shot at
the word from the spelling."

61. **And halt his feeste solempne and so ryche.** The accent in
'solempne' falling on the second syllable (cp. l. 111.), the *e*- final in
'feeste' must here be silent, while that in 'solempne' is sounded
before a vowel in virtue of the cæsural pause.

66. **At every cours the ordre of hire servyse.** The *New Eng.
Dict.* defines 'course,' in this sense, as a division of a meal, the set
of dishes placed upon the table at one time, and quotes from the
romance of *Coer de Lion* (c. 1325):

> "Fro kechene come the fryste cours
> With pypes and tiumpes and tabours,"

which sufficiently explains "the ordre of hire servyse."

67. **hir strange sewes.** "A sewer was an officer so called from
his placing the dishes upon the table. *Asseour*, Fr. from *asseoir*, to
place." In the establishment of the king's household there are still
four *Gentlemen Sewers*. *Sewes* here seem to mean *dishes*, from the
same original; as *assiette* in French still signifies a little dish or plate.
See Gower, *Conf. Aman.*:

> "The flesh, whan it was so to-hewe
> She taketh, and maketh thereof a sewe."
> (Tyrwhitt's note.)

68. **Ne of hir swannes, ne of hire heronsewes.** These birds
continued to be considered dainties long after Chaucer's time.
Henry VIII.'s proclamation of 21st May, 1544, fixed the price of
"the best swanne" at not above five shillings, and "heronshewes"
at "xviijᵈ the pece."

69-70. **Eek in that lond,** etc., an allusion to the strange food,
such as dogs, rats, and horses, which not only Marco Polo, but Carpini, Vincent of Beauvais, William de Rubruquis, Mandeville, and
other writers represent the Tartars as eating.

73. **I wol nat taryen yow, for it is pryme.** 'Prime' is properly
the first hour or first division of the day after sunrise, or its average
equivalent, 6 a.m. But in Chaucer 'fully pryme' and 'pryme
large' mean 9 a.m., 'half way pryme' 7-30, and 'prime' in general
the time approaching 9 o'clock. This is one of the 'notes of time'
by which we trace Chaucer's pilgrims on their road to Canterbury.

75. **Unto my firste,** etc., I will return to my first subject.

78. **hir thynges pleye.** The word 'thing' is used by Chaucer
with various special meanings: to "make a thyng" (*Prologue*, 325),
is 'to draw a legal document'; in the *Legend of Good Women*, "he
useth things for to make" is said of Chaucer's own verse-making; in

the *Knight's Tale* (A 2293), "dide her thinges" means 'made her offerings or sacrifice'; in the *Shipman's Tale* (B 1281), "sey his thinges" = 'read his appointed prayers.' Here the reference must be to musical compositions. The line should perhaps be scanned :

Hérk | nynge his | mynstrales | hir thyng | es pleye.

79. bord. The typical medieval table was a board placed, when needed, on movable trestles. A fixed table was called a "table dormant" (*Prologue*, 353).

81. a steede of bras : for notes as to these marvels, see the Introduction.

85. up he rideth to the heighe bord : in Guy of Warwick, when Guy beards the Sultan in his pavilion, we are told :

" Guy rode forth, and spake no word
Till he came to the soudans bord."

At coronation banquets in Westminster Hall the champion of England used to ride fully armed into the hall, and there deliver his challenge to all who should contest the king's right.

92. By ordre. Precedence was a very important matter in Chaucer's days. In the *Prologue* (743-46) he thinks it necessary to ask forgiveness.

" Al have I nat set folk in hir degree ·
Heere in this tale, as that they sholde stonde."

93. obeisaunce, the Harley MS. reads *observaunce.*

95. Gawayn, with his olde curteisye. Sir Gawain was the son of King Lot of Orkney and nephew of King Arthur. In Malory's *Morte d'Arthur* not much stress is laid on Gawain's courtesy; but in *Sir Gawain and the Green Knight*, when it is known that it is he who has come to the castle, " Each said softly to his fellow, ' Now shall we see courteous bearing, and the manner of speech befitting courts. What charm lieth in gentle speech shall we learn without asking, since here we have welcomed the fine father of courtesy'" (Miss Weston's Paraphrase, p. 34). " Gawayn the curtesse and Cay the crabbed " (*Thersites*, l. 130) passed into a proverb.

96. come ageyn out of fairye. For this assignment of the Knights of the Round Table to fairyland, compare the opening of the *Wife of Bath's Tale* :

" In tholde dayes of the Kyng Arthour,
Of which that Britons speken greet honour,
All was this land fulfild of faïrye."

105-106. stile ... style. For this repetition of the same sound in two different meanings by way of a rhyme, cp. ll. 203, 204, and *Prologue*, 17, 18 :

" The hooly blissful martir for to seke
That hem hath holpen whan that they were seeke."

Such rhymes have long been rejected in English verse, but they are recognized as permissible in French.

110. **The kyng of Arable and of Inde.** The maker of the Enchanted Horse in the *Arabian Nights* is an Indian.

114. **al redy at youre heeste.** The Harley MS. reads "redy at al *his* heste."

115. **This steede of bras**: see Introduction.

116. **o day natureel**, as opposed to the 'artificial' day, from sunrise to sunset, the length of which (and of its hours) varies.

118. **in droghte or elles shoures.** Chaucer insists again on the steed's indifference to weather in l. 121, but it is not unfair to suggest that here he was thinking chiefly of a rhyme.

129. **wayted many a constellacioun.** The maker of the horse watched the stars to set about his work at an astrologically propitious moment. This watching for fortunate times was the chief feature in the "magik naturel" to which Chaucer often alludes. Cp. the remarks about the "Doctour of Phisik" (*Prologue*, ll. 414-22); also *Man of Law's Tale*, ll. 309-14; and *Franklin's Tale*, ll. 1261-96.

131. **knew ful many a seel, and many a bond.** The use of magical seals dates back from legends of Solomon, of whom we read in the *Arabian Nights* (Burton, v. 1), "He held sway over Jinn and beast and bird, and was wont when he was wroth with one of the Marids to shut him in a cucurbite (bottle) of brass, and stopping its mouth on him with lead, whereon he impressed his seal-ring, to cast him into the sea." 'Bond' may be used either of a deed binding a spirit to do him service, or a fetter imprisoning a spirit till it was obedient.

132. **This mirrour**: see Introduction.

146. **The vertu of the ryng**: see Introduction.

156. **This naked swerd**: see Introduction.

165. **Stróke hym in the wounde.** For other lines beginning with a single accented syllable for the first foot, see ll. 346 and 390. The Ellesmere MS. reads *strike* for *stroke*.

171. **as stille as.** Only the Harley MS. makes the line run smoothly by reading *as stille as*, the other MSS. omitting the first *as*. In a later writer we might think that the slow movement of a defective line was meant to illustrate the sense, but it is not probable that Chaucer intended this.

174. **roially y-fet**, *i.e.* sent for with great ceremony.

193. **a steede of Lumbardye.** Tyrwhitt notes that "there is a patent" in Rymer, 2 E, ii., *De dextrariis in Lumbardiâ emendis*, 'about buying steeds in Lombardy.'

195. **a gentil Poilleys courser.** · The word 'courser' used now for a fleet horse, until about the time of Dryden meant especially

a horse ridden in battle or tournament. Cp. R. Johnson's *Kingdom and Commonwealth* (1630, quoted in *New Eng. Dict.*): "The courser of Naples...though he be not so swift as the Spanish Genet, yet is he better able to indure travail, and to beare the weight of Armor." *Gentil* here means 'high bred,' 'of good stock.' Tyrwhitt notes that a horse of Apulia in old French was usually called *Poille*, and quotes a playful passage from Richard of Armagh, who contrasts the "mulus Hispaniae" and "dextrarius Apuliae" with the English 'Thom-ass,' *i.e.* S. Thomas of Canterbury.

207. **the Pegasee**: the form is explained by the side-note, "equus Pegaseus" (the Pegasean horse), in the Ellesmere and other MSS. Pegasus was the winged steed of Bellerophon.

209. **the Grekes hors Synoun**, the horse of the Greek, Sinon, *i.e.* the Wooden Horse about which Sinon told the Trojans his lying story. For the order of the words, cp. *Dethe of Blaunche*, l. 282: "The kynges metyng Pharao," *i.e.* the dreaming of the king Pharaoh. Even as late as Malory's *Morte d'Arthur* we find such a construction as "I am the lordes doghter of this castel" for 'I am the daughter of the lord of this castle.'

211. **in thise olde geestes.** Chaucer's knowledge of the siege of Troy was derived from Virgil's *Aeneid* (book ii.), and from the *Historia Trojana* of Guido delle Colonne.

213. **som men of armes**, as in the Trojan horse.

218. **An apparence, y-maad by som magyk.** The best commentary on this line is a passage from the *Franklin's Tale* (F 1139-51):

> "For I am siker that ther be sciences
> By whiche men maken diverse apparences,
> Swiche as these subtile tregetoures pleye ;
> For ofte at feestes have I wel herd seye
> That tregetours withinne an halle large
> Have maad come in a water and a barge,
> And in the halle rowen up and doun.
> Somtyme hath semed come a grym leoun,
> And somtyme floures sprynge as in a mede ;
> Somtyme a vyne, and grapes white and rede ;
> Somtyme a castel, al of lym and stoon,
> And whan hym lyked voyded it anoon—
> Thus semed it to every mannes sighte."

219. **jogelours**, the 'tregetours' of the quotation from the *Franklin's Tale.*

226. **the maistre tour**, the master or chief tower. The Ellesmere and Cambridge MSS. read "the hye tour" as in l. 176.

231. **in Rome was swich oon.** In some way, not quite satisfactorily explained, out of the fame of the poet Virgil there grew up a number of medieval legends about a Virgil who was a magician. One of the inventions attributed to him was a magic mirror in which

the Emperor of Rome could see what his enemies were doing thirty miles off. The story of this is told by Gower in his *Confessio Amantis*, and is alluded to in the romance of Cleomades (see Introduction) which resembles the *Squire's Tale* in so many points.

232. **Alocen**, Alhazen, an Arab astronomer of the 11th century.

Vitulon, Vitellio, a Polish astronomer of the 13th century.

233. **Aristotle**, the Greek philosopher, who lived B.C. 384-332.

that writen in hir lyves, that wrote in their lifetimes.

238. **Thelophus the kyng**, Telephus of Mysia, whom Achilles, when on his way to Troy, wounded with his spear. He overtook Achilles at Argos, and with the help of Clytemnestra made him heal the wound with rust or splinters from the spear which gave it.

239. **And of Achilles for his queynte spere**, they talked of Achilles because of his wonderful spear. Instead of *for* the Ellesmere and Cambridge MSS. read *with*.

250. **he Moyses and kyng Salomon**. The belief in Moses as a magician sprang from the wonders he performed to break down Pharaoh's refusal to let the Israelites go; the supernatural gift of wisdom to Solomon gave him a similar fame. According to Mr. Clouston, the "so-called ring of Moses" caused its wearer "to forget his love, in fact everything; hence it was called the Ring of Oblivion."

263. **the angle meridional**. The four angles answered to the 1st, 4th, 7th, and 10th Houses (see *Chaucer's Astrology*, § 5), the southern angle being the last of the four. On March 15th the sun would pass through this House between 10 a.m. and noon.

265. **The gentil Leon, with his Aldrian**, or Aldiran, the star marking the fore-paws of the constellation Leo. According to Prof. Skeat Leo would begin to ascend on March 15th about noon, but the star Aldiran would not be visible till nearly two o'clock.

272. **Venus children**, lovers.

273. **For in the Fyssh hir lady sat ful hye**. Venus has her "exaltation" in the sign of Pisces. See note on *Chaucer's Astrology*, § 6.

274. **eye**, the true spelling in Chaucer's day is *yë*.

279. **That is nat able a dul man to devyse**. In this and the three following lines Chaucer is thinking of himself, not of his Squire, of whom in the *Prologue* (l. 92) he had expressly said, "He was as fresh as is the month of May." We might imagine from this passage that the *Squire's Tale* was written independently of the *Canterbury Tales*, but the note of time in l. 73 seems to show the contrary.

287. **No man but Launcelet**, Launcelot, the bravest and most courteous of Arthur's knights, and the secret lover of Queen Guinevere.

C

292. Chambre of parements. Tyrwhitt notes that "*Chambre de parement* is translated by Cotgreave (in his *French-English Dictionary*) the presence-chamber, and *lit de parement* a bed of state. *Parements* originally signified all sorts of ornamental furniture or clothes, from *parer*, Fr. to adorn."

297. they soupen al by day. In *Sir Gawain and the Green Knight* Gawain reaches the castle in the morning of Christmas Eve, dresses, has dinner, goes to service, after which spices and wine are served, followed by merry talk and bed. Here the knight with his presents arrives after the third course of dinner; dinner is over about 2 p.m. ; after dinner comes dancing followed by spices and wine, and then by a service and supper by daylight, *i.e.* about 6 p.m. After supper the horse is inspected, and the revels resumed and kept up far into the night.

299. that a kynges feeste : the Hengwrt and three minor MSS. mend the metre of this line by reading "that *at* a kynges feeste," and with this reading it is said that "hath plentee" in the next line is to be explained as an adaptation of the French construction *il y a*. But in the absence of other English parallels to such a construction the reading can hardly be accepted against the authority of the Ellesmere, Cambridge, and Harleian MSS.

302. At after. The *New Eng. Dict.* gives the following note : "*At after*, prep., used where we should now use *after* alone to indicate time when. The *after* may in some cases belong to the sb. following; cf. *after-noon*." The instances quoted from other authors are "at after matins," "at after midnight," and "at after noon."

306. grete sege of Troie, cp. l. 20.

316. Ye mooten trille a pyne, stant in his ere. The omission of the relative (*stant*, for which standeth) is uncommon in Chaucer.

346. Til wel ny, etc. : for the metre, cp. l. 165.

352. blood was in his domynacioun. According to the *Shepherd's Kalendar* (Pynson's ed. 1506) the four complexions of man are the sanguine, choleric, melancholy, and phlegmatic. "Syxe houres after mydnyght blode hath ye maystry, and in the .vi. houres after noone coloure reyneth, and .vi. howres after none reyneth melancholy, and .vi. houres afore mydnyght reygneth the fleme." According to a quotation of Tyrwhitt's from the *De Natura* of the pseudo-Galen, the domination of blood lasted from the ninth hour of the night to the third of the day.

360. it was pryme large, fully 9 o'clock. See note to l. 73.

374. hir maistresse, *i.e.* her duenna or chaperone.

376. that been gladly wyse, that gladly show off their wisdom. Grammatically, the subject to 'answerde' is 'thise olde wommen,' but the real subject is, of course, 'hir maistresse.'

385. the yonge sonne. The sun is called 'young' because he was supposed to begin his annual course at the vernal equinox, the Ram or Aries (cp. l. 51) being the first 'sign' into which he enters. Into this he came, in Chaucer's time, on March 12th, and on March 16th (the story opens on the 15th, see l. 47) at his rising he would be passing from the 4th degree to the 5th. See *Chaucer's Astrology*, § 2.

387. Noon hyer was he, etc., the sun was not more than four degrees above the horizon, *i.e.* had only risen about a quarter of an hour.

388. esily a pas. To walk 'apace,' or 'at a pace,' now means to walk quickly, but in Chaucer's day it had the opposite sense of 'at a footpace' (cp. *Prologue*, 825, "and forth we riden a litel more than paas"), and so 'slowly.' Cp. *Troilus*, ii. 624-28 :

> " And wounded was his hors and gan to blede,
> On which he rod a pas ful softely."

392. a trench, literally 'a cutting' (Fr. *trancher*), a path cut through the wood.

401-405. The knotte, etc.   The 'it' in l. 401 is resumptive. The bald meaning of the passage is : 'If the plot, which is the chief object of every tale, is retarded till the pleasure of those who for a long time have been listening to catch it grows cold, the agreeableness of it becomes continually less, from the satiety produced by the teller's long-windedness.'

409. Amydde a tree fordrye.   There seems no reason to identify this with the famous '*Arbre sec*' or 'Dry Tree,' mentioned by medieval travellers, which was said to have dried up at the time of Christ's crucifixion.

417. ever in oon, always in one way, incessantly.   Cp. *Knight's Tale* (A 1771) : "they wepen ever in oon."

419. nys tigre noon, ne crueel beest : text from the Harleian MS.; EC, "nys tigre ne noon so crueel beest"; Hengwrt, "nys tigre ne so cruel beest"; Corp. Pet. Laus., "ne was tygre ne cruel beest."

425. swich another of fairnesse.   For this use of 'of,' meaning 'with reference to,' 'in respect of,' cp. *Parlement of Foules*, 298-301 :

> " Tho was I war wher that ther sat a quene
> That *as of light* the somer-sunne shene
> Passeth the sterre, right so over mesure
> She fairer was than any creature."

428. A faucon peregryn.   Tyrwhitt quotes a passage from the *Tresor de Brunet Latin*, which tells us "the second kind is the falcon, which is called *pelerins*, because no one finds its nest, and so it is taken elsewhere as if on pilgrimages ; and it is very easy to bring up, very courteous, and brave, and of good manner." ("La seconde lignie est faucons, que hom apele *pelerins*, par ce que nus ne trove son ni ; ains est pris autresi come en *pelerinage* ; et est mult legiers a norrir, et mult cortois, et vaillans, et de bone maniere.")

434. she understood wel every thyng. The rhythm of the verse shows that 'wel' must be taken with 'every thyng' rather than with 'understond.' The meaning is thus not 'she understood everything well,' but 'she understood quite everything.' Cp. *Legend of Good Women*, 10-11 :

> " But God forbede but men shulde leve
> Wel more thyng than men han seen with eye."

447. If it be for to telle, if it be lawful or suitable to tell. Cp. *Mars*, 74 : "But for his nature was not for to wepe."

455. ire. The Ellesmere reading *love* seems at first sight much simpler, but anger at broken faith and dread of such treachery go very well together, whereas if we read *love* we must take *drede* to stand for 'fear' absolutely, which is out of keeping with the passage.

458. as dooth : for this use of 'as' heralding an imperative to express a wish, cp. *Doctor's Tale* (C 66), "As dooth me right upon this pitous bille"; *Miller's Tale* (A 3777), "As lene it me."

461. ferde with hymself : 'faren' often means 'behave' (cp. l. 621), but it means also to prosper or succeed, ill or well (cp. *Canon's Yeoman's Tale*, G 1417, "So faren ye that multiplie, I seye"). Thus 'faren with' means to 'succeed in relation to.' Cp. *Miller's Tale* (A 3457), "so ferde another clerk with astromye," *i.e.* 'this is what another clerk got from astronomy.' The sense here is 'that was so piteously treated by himself.'

465. And ... If ... I ... knew, etc. We should expect either '*for* if I knew I would,' etc., or '*and* if I shall learn ... I will.'

471. To heele with youre hurtes, with which to heal your hurts. Cp. l. 641.

476. Unto the tyme she gan, *i.e.* until the time she should begin.

479. That pitee renneth soone in gentil herte : this beautiful line occurs four times in Chaucer. Cp. *Knight's Tale* (A 1761), *Merchant's Tale* (E 1986), *Legend of Good Women* (503).

482. auctoritee, the usual word for the opinion of writers of repute.

491. As by the whelpe chastysed is the leoun, a proverb. Prof. Skeat appositely compares *Othello*, ii. 3, 372, "a punishment more in policy than in malice ; even so as one would beat his offenceless dog to affright an imperious lion." The 'whipping boy' who was educated with a little prince, and whipped for the prince's faults, was a good example of this theory. The Ellesmere and Hengwrt MSS. read *chasted* for *chastysed*.

496. as she to water wolde, as if she would melt, or dissolve in tears ; for 'wolde' cp. l. 617, "and to the wode he wole,"

506. **Al were he,** although he was. Our modern distinction by which we use the indicative after words like 'although,' to express a fact, and the subjunctive to express a belief, was not observed by Chaucer.

512. **hit,** the contracted form for 'hideth.'

515-16. The Harleian MS. reads *observaunce* instead of *obeissaunces,* and in the next line, "Under subtil colour and aqueyntaunce."

526. **his corouned malice.** For 'corouned' in this sense of 'perfect,' 'consummate,' cp. Burton's *Anatomy of Melancholy* : " 'Tis a crowned medicine which must be kept in secret."

527. **For-fered of his deeth, as thoughte me,** rather a loose construction, 'greatly afraid that, as it seemed to me, he would die.'

537. **A trewe wight and a theef thenken nat oon,** an honest man and a thief do not see alike. Neither the source of the proverb nor any close parallel to it has been found.

542. Prof. Skeat mends the metre of this line by reading "As he swoor he his herte yaf to me."

548. **Jason,** who deserted Medea, by whose aid he had won the Golden Fleece, for Creusa.

Parys of Troye, who deserted Oenone for Helen.

550. **Syn Lameth was,** etc. See *Genesis* iv. 19. The Wyf of Bath in her Prologue asks,

"What rekketh me thogh folk seye vileynye
Of shrewed Lameth, and his bigamye?" (D 53, 54)

and in *Anelyda and Arcyte* he is celebrated in a whole stanza (ll. 148-54) :

"But nathelesse, gret wonder was hit noon
Thogh he were fals, for hit is kynde of man,
Sith Lamek was, that is so longe agoon,
To been in love as fals as ever he can ;
He was the firste fader that began
To loven two, and was in bigamye.
And he found tentes first, but if men lye."

553. **by twenty thousand part,** by the twenty thousandth part.

555. **Ne were worthy unbokele his galoche,** a reminiscence of "The latchet of whose shoes I am not worthy to stoop down and unloose." (*Mark* i. 7.) The *galoche* was a sort of patten.

559. **Til any womman:** this Northern form *til* is used by Chaucer before a vowel. Cp. *Prologue*, 179-80 :

"Ne that a Monk whan he is recchelees
Is likned til a fissh that is waterlees."

So "til a grove," *Knight's Tale* (A 1478).

560. **kembde at point-devys**, arranged to a nicety.

579. **Wher me was wo, that is no questioun**: in modern English, 'you need not ask whether I was grieved.'

593. **That I made vertu of necessitee.** S. Jerome in his Epistles (*Ep.* 52, § 6) writes, "Fac de necessitate virtutem"; and in Chaucer's favourite *Roman de la Rose* (l. 14,058) we have the phrase, "sil ne fait de necessite virtu."

596. **Seint John to borwe**, Saint John being security. For the use of the dative, cp. "his nekke lith to wedde" (*i.e.* in pledge), *Knight's Tale*, A 1218, and "Ech of hem had leyd his feith to borwe," *ib.* 1622. It is usually said that the S. John is S. John the divine, who praises truth in his Epistles; but it is at least possible that the reference may be to S. John Baptist, with whose midsummer festival many lovers' rites were connected.

601. **Whan he hath al wel-seyd, thanne hath he doon**, he protests beautifully and does nothing more.

602. **bihoveth hire a ful long spoon**, etc. Cp. *Tempest*, ii. 2, where Stephano says of Caliban, "This is a devil and no monster. I will leave him. I have no long spoon." For *hire* the Harleian and three other MSS. read *hym*.

604. **he moste forth his weye**, he must go forth on his way. Both *must* and *forth* can be used with an ellipse of *go*. Cp. *Hous of Fame*, 187, "he moste into Itaille"; *Troilus*, v. 5, "Criseyde moste out of the toun"; and Robert of Brunne, "No lenger suld thai byde, bot forth and stand to chance."

608. **thilke text ... That "Alle thyng repeirynge to his kynde,"** etc. From Boethius, *De Consolatione Philosophiae*, book iii., met. 2, translated by Chaucer: "Alle thynges seken ayen to hir propre cours, and alle thynges rejoysen hem of hir retornynge ayen to hir nature." The simile in ll. 611, etc., is from the same source: "the janglinge brid that syngeth on the heigh branches, and after is enclosed in a streyte cage, al thoghe that the pleyinge bysynes of men yeveth hem honyed drynkes and large metes, with swete studyes [Chaucer's translation of 'dulci studio'], yit natheles yif thilke bryd skippynge out of hir streyte cage seith the agreable schadwes of the wodes, sche defouleth with hir feet hir metes i-schad, and seketh mornynge oonly the wode, and twytereth desyrynge the wode with hir swete voys." Cp. also *Manciples Tale* (H 163-174).

613-615. **hir ... his.** Chaucer changes from the plural to the singular.

617. **to the wode he wole**, cp. l. 496.

638. **Now kan nat Canacee but herbes delve**, Canacee can now do nothing but dig herbs. For *nat ... but*, cp. l. 391.

641. **To heelen with this hauk**, cp. l. 471.

644. **veluettes blewe ... peynted grene.** For the contrast of

blue and green as the colours typical of faithfulness and incon-
stancy, cp. the *Balade against Women Unconstant*, attributed to
Chaucer, ll. 6, 7 :

" To newe thygne your lust is ay so kene ;
In stede of blew, thus may ye we e all grene."

649, 650. The MSS. give these lines in the reverse order. The
transposition was proposed by Tyrwhitt.

655. as the storie telleth us. An explicit reference like this
surely proves that Chaucer took his plot from some earlier writer,
and did not piece it together himself from stray hints in books like
the travels of Marco Polo.

667. Cambalo, apparently *not* Canacee's brother, though bearing
the same name.

671, 672. Appollo. The house of Mercury is in the sign Gemini,
which the chariot of the Sun would not enter until the middle of
May, nearly two months after the beginning of the story.

697, 698. moot tellen atte leste A tale or two, etc. In the
General Prologue Harry Bailey laid down (l. 792) that each pilgrim
"in this viage shal telle tales tweye," and all the subsequent refer-
ences agree with this. But ll. 793, 794 of the *Prologue*, which read
so much like an interpolation, oblige each pilgrim to tell four
stories, two going and two returning.

ILLUSTRATIONS OF CHAUCER'S GRAMMAR FROM THE SQUIRE'S TALE.

SUBSTANTIVES.

I. **Examples of Substantives possessing a fully-sounded e- final independent of inflection.**

(a) *Words of French Origin*: Cage, 613; cause, 185, 466; eloquence, 678; gentilesse, 694; joye, 368; place, 578. But in l. 186 *place* is monosyllabic.

(b) *Words of English Origin*: Herte (O.E. heorte), 120, 483; kyte (cyta), 624; knotte (cnotta), 401; sone (sunu), 688; sonne (sunne), 53, 170; sorwe (sorg), 495; steede (steda), 170; tale (talu), 6, 168; trouthe (treowth), 627; wille (willa), 1; yowthe (geoguth), 675.

Besides the dissyllabic *wille*, Chaucer also uses the monosyllabic *wyl* (568, 569, 704). In ll. 31, 48, 124 the apparent silence of the e final in *sone*, *sonne*, and *steede* is explainable as due to its occurrence at the cæsural pause.

II. **Inflections.**

(a) *Genitive singular in* -es: Beddes, 643; Goddes, 464; haukes, 632; kynges, 299; someres, 64; willes, 568.

(b) *Datives in* -e: Borwe, 596; while, 590.

NOTE.—*Halle* in *halle-dore*, l. 80, may be intended as a genitive feminine, and *halle* in l. 86 as a dative, but as *halle* is the M.E. form in the nominative also, we cannot quote these as survivals of old inflections.

(c) *Plurals in* -es: Bookes, 235; heddes, 358; knyghtes, 69; lordes, 304; rynges, 249; thynges, 78; wordes, 103; wynges, 208.

In l. 706 *wittes* is dissyllabic; in l. 203, 'as many heddes as manye wittes ther been.' We can only give it its full value by omitting 'ther,' an omission not supported by any of the seven manuscripts.

(d) *Plurals in* -en: Asshen, 255; been, 204.

40

(*e*) *Plurals without inflection*: Folk, 203; pound, 683; wynter, 63.

ADJECTIVES.

I. **Examples of adjectives possessing a fully-sounded e- final independent of inflection.**

Fremde, 429; fresshe, 384; longe, 444.
NOTE.—For *fresshe* as a dissyllable compare 'fresshe Beautee' (Pity, 39); for *longe*, cp. 'longe tyme' (*Dethe of Blaunche*, 380). But Chaucer is not consistent as regards this e- final in adjectives.

II. **Definite forms making singular in -e.**

The firste man, 552; the grete sege, 306; the heighe bord, 85; my trewe herte, 541.

III. **Indefinite, without inflection.**

A brood mirour, 82; a greet route, 382; so heigh reverence, 545; a trew wight, 537; yong, fressh, and strong in armes desirous, 23.

IV. **Plurals in -e.**

Olde poetries, 206; olde geestes, 211; queynte mirours, 234; swiche thynges, 227.

V. **Genitive plural in -er, -re, -ra.**

Alderfirst (first of all), 550.

VI. **Comparatives.**

Note the form 'badder,' 226.

ADVERBS.

I. **In -e-**

Faste, 504; loude, 55; soore, 258.

II. **In -ly.**

Deliciously, 79; openly, 136; sikerly, 180; sodeynly, 80.

III. **In -ely.**

Boldely, 581; softely, 636.

IV. **Comparatives.**

Note the form 'bet,' 600.

VERBS.

I. **Present Indicative.**

(*a*) *1st sing. in* -e: I trowe, 451.
(*b*) *3rd sing. in* -eth, -th: Amounteth, 108; cesseth, 258;

demeth, 221 ; gladeth, 393 ; happeth, 592 ; listeth, 689 ;
dooth, 123 ; fleeth, 149 ; lith, 322.

(c) *Contracted form of* 3rd *sing.*: Byt, 291 ; halt, 61 ; hit,
512 ; sit, 77 ; stant, 170.

(d) *Plural in* -en, -e : Dauncen, 272 ; demen, 261 ;
drawen, 252 ; knowen, 235 ; shapen, 214 ; sownen, 270 ;
jangle, 261 ; speke, 244.

(e) *Plural in* -eth : Sowneth, 517.

II. **Past Indicative.** 1*st and* 3*rd sing.*:

(a) *Strong.* Baar, 433 ; bad, 348 ; cam, 181 ; fil, 473 ;
glood, 393 ; wan, 662 ; yaf, 533.

(b) *Weak.* (i.) Dyde, 11 ; kembde, 560 ; lakked, 16 ;
peynted, 560 ; felte, 566 ; kepte, 18 ; mente, 108. (ii.) broghte,
210 ; thoughte, 566 ; wroghte, 128.

III. **Imperative Present.**

(a) 2*nd sing.*:
Strong. Com, 464.
Weak. (i.) Sey, 2 ; (ii.) trille, 328.

(b) 2*nd plur.*: Beth, 598 ; cherisseth, 353 ; dooth, 458.

IV. **Infinitives in** -en, -n, -e.

(a) Fallen, 134 ; percen, 237 ; taryen, 73 ; tellen, 63 ;
doon, 323 ; goon, 200 ; aryse, 262 ; heere, 144 ; rebelle, 5 ;
telle, 6.

(b) *Gerundial* : To fleen, 122 ; to seyne, 314 ; to telle, 34 ;
to were, 147 ; to wynne, 214.

V. **Past Participles.**

Strong. Doon, 129 ; y-goon, 293 ; knowe, 215 ; y-bore,
326 ; y-drawe, 326.
Weak. (a) Cleped, 12 ; herd, 235 ; remewed, 181 ;
y-glewed, 182 ; y-harded, 245. (b) Toold, 58.

GLOSSARY.

NOTE.—y *in the middle of a word is arranged as* i.

abreyde, 3 *s. pret.* started, awoke, 477 (O.E. *abregdan*).

abrood, *adv.* abroad, spread out, 441.

accordant, *adj.* agreeable to, 103.

adoun, *adv.* down, 351.

affecciouns, *sb. pl.* desires, 55.

after, *adv.* afterwards, 188 ; *prep.* after, according to, 47.

agayn, ageyn, *adv.* again, 96, 331 ; *prep.* against, 6 ; in the presence, at the approach of, 53, 142.

ago, *p.p.* agone, gone, 626 (*var.*).

al, *adj.* all, 24, 34 ; **alle,** *dat. s.* 15.

al, *adv.* although, 155, 506 ; **al be it,** albeit, although it so be that, 105.

alderfirst, first of all, 550 (the prefix is the old genitive plural *aller, alra*; cp. *allerbest, alderlevest*).

algates, *adv.* at all events, anyhow, 246.

allowe, 1 *s. pres.* praise, 676.

amende, *v.* amend, improve, 97, 197.

amys, *adv.* amiss, wrongly, 7.

amounteth, 3 *sing. pres.* amounts to, 108 (O. Fr. *amonter*, climb up, ascend, attain to).

anoon, *adv.* anon, at once, 172, 312, 328 (O.E. *on âne*, in one).

aperceyvynges, *sb. pl.* perceptions, observations, 286.

apert, *adj.* open, 531 (O. Fr. *apert*, Lat. *apertum*).

appalled, *p.p.* made pale or feeble, 365 (O. Fr. *apalir*).

apparence, *sb.* appearance, vision, dream, 218.

aright, *adv.* rightly, 336.

armure, *sb.* armour, 158 (O. Fr. *armeüre, armure*, Lat. *armitura*).

as, introducing an imperative, 458.

asshen, *sb. pl.* ashes, 255 (the plural in *s* is used by Ormin).

aswowne, *adverb. phrase,* in a swoon, fainting, 474.

at after, *prep.* after, 302 (see note).

atte, at the, 445.

auctoritee, *sb.* authority, 482 (Lat. *auctoritas*).

aventures, *sb. pl.* adventures, 659 (Fr. *aventure*, Lat. *adventura*, the *d* in which begins to re-appear in the English form towards the end of the 15th century, but was not common till the second half of the 16th).

43

awook, 3 *s. pret.* awoke, 367.
axeth, 3 *s. pres.* asks, 309.

baar, 3 *s. pret.* bare, carried, 433.
bacheler, *sb.* a young knight (Prov. *bacalar,* It. *baccalare,* Fr. *bachelier*; the ultimate derivation is doubtful).
badder, *adj. comp.* worse, 224.
bak, *sb.* back, 126.
barm, *sb.* bosom, 631.
batailles, *sb. pl.* battles, 659.
beek, *sb.* beak, 418.
been, *sb. pl.* bees, 204.
been, *v.* to be, 192; 3 *pl. pres.* are, 203, 213, 222, 294.
beest, *sb.* beast, 264.
benigne, *adj.* kindly, favourable, 21, 52.
benignytee, *sb.* kindliness, 486.
beren, *v.* to bear, carry, 119.
beth, 2 *pl. imperat.* be, 598.
bettre, *adj.* better, 102.
bifel, 3 *s. pret.* befell, happened, 42.
biforn, *prep.* and *adv.* before, 79, 339.
bigan, 3 *s. pret.* began, 312.
biholde, *v.* to behold, 87.
bileve, *v.* remain, 583 (O. E. *belǣfan*).
bisy, *adj.* busy, careful, 509.
bisily, *adv.* busily, eagerly, 88.
byt, 3 *s. pres.* biddeth, bids, 291.
bitwix, bitwixe, *prep.* between, 317, 333.
boote, *sb.* advantage, remedy, 154 (O. E. *bót*).
bord, *sb.* table, 79, 85, 98, 262.
borwe, *sb.* pledge; **to borwe,** as a pledge, 596 (O. E. *borg*).
bras, *sb.* brass, 81, 115.
bryd, *sb.* bird; **briddes,** *pl.* 611.
brydel, *sb.* bridle, 340.
brood, *adj.* broad, 82, 191, 394.
but, *conj.* unless, 361.

cam, 3 *s. pret.* came, 81, 89.
certes, *adv.* certainly, assuredly, 2, 196.
cesseth, 3 *s. pres.* ceases, 257.
chambre, *sb.* chamber, room, 172, 269.
charge, *sb.* weighty matter, 359 (Fr. *charge,* late Lat. *carica,* a load or burden).
chasted, *p.p.* corrected, chastised, reading of E² in 491 (O. Fr. *·hastier,* Lat. *castigare.* The forms *chasten, chastened* date from the 16th century).
cheere, *sb.* countenance, aspect, outward show, 103, 507, 545 (O. Fr. *chiere,* late Lat. *cara,* face).
cherisseth, 2 *pl. imperat.* cherish, 353.
citee, *sb.* city, 46, 214.
clepen, *v.* to call; **cleped,** 3 *s. pret.* called, 374; **cleped,** *p.p.* called, 12, 31 (O. E. *clipian*).
clymben, *v.* o climb, 106.
colerik, *adj.* choleric, 51.
colours, *sb. pl.* "rhetorical modes or figures, ornaments of style or diction, embellishments" (*N.E.D.,* where no earlier instance is quoted).
com, 2 *s. imperat.* come, 464.
comen, *p.p.* come, 96 (*var.*).
commune, *adj.* common, popular, 107.
composiciouns, *sb. pl.* compositions, arrangements, 229.
comunly, *adv.* commonly, usually, 221.
conceyved, *p.p.* conceived, understood, 336.
condescende, *v.* settle down to, 407.
constellacioun, *sb.* constellation, 129.
contenaunce, *sb.* countenance, aspect, 93; **contenaunces,** *pl.* 284.

contree, *sb.* country, 318.
corage, *sb.* heart, courage, 22.
corouned, *p.p.* crowned, consummate, 526.
corps, *sb.* corpse, body, 519.
cours, *sb.* course, service (in a meal), 66, 76.
courser, *sb.* a charger or battlehorse, 195, 310.
craft, *sb.* art, secret workmanship, 185, 249.
cryen, *v.* to cry, 46.

dar, 1 *s. pres.* dare, 36.
dauncen, 3 *pl. pres.* dance, 272.
dede, *sb.* deed, 456.
deed, *p.p.* dead, 287.
deere, *adj.* dear, 272.
dees, *sb. pl.* dice, 690.
deyde, 3 *s. pret.* died, 438.
deynte, *adj.* dainty, delicious, 70.
deyntee, *sb.* delight, 681; deyntees, *pl.* dainties, 301.
deys, *sb.* dais, raised platform, 59.
delve, *v.* to dig, 638.
deme, 1 *s. pres.* deem, judge, suppose, 44; demeth, 3 *s. pres.* 221; demen, 3 *pl. pres.* 261.
dere, *v.* to harm, 240 (O.E. *derian*).
desert, *sb.* merit, deserving, 532.
desirous, *adj.* eager, 23.
despende, *v.* spend, squander, 690.
despit, *sb.* despite, scorn, 650. (O. Fr. *despit*, Lat. *despectus*, lit. a looking down on).
destruccioun, *sb.* destruction, 210.
devyse, devysen, *v.* to describe, 65, 279, 282; devyse, 3 *pl. pres.* 261 (O. Fr. *deviser*, late Lat. *divisare*, to divide, so to mark in detail).

dyde, 3 *s. pret.* died, 11.
discryve, discryven, *v.* to describe, 424, 40 (O. Fr. *descrivre*, Lat. *describere*: the *v* form was supplanted by *b* in England in the 16th century, but survived in Scotch to the time of Burns).
dissymulynges, *sb. pl.* dissemblings, 285.
diverse, *adj. pl.* different, various, 202, 270.
diversely, *adv.* differently, variously, 202.
doghter, *sb.* daughter, 32.
domynacioun, *sb.* domination, predominance, 352.
doom, *sb.* judgment, 677.
doon, *v.* to do, make, cause, 46, 323, 334; dooth, 3 *s. pres.* does, 123; 2 *s. imperat.* do, 458; doon, *p.p.* done, 297.
doughty, *adj.* brave, 11 (O.E. *dyhtig*; cp. Mod. Germ. *tüchtig*).
doun, *adv.* down, 169, 323.
doutes, *sb. pl.* doubts, 220.
drawen, 3 *pl. pres.* draw, remove, 252.
drede, *sb.* fear, 286.
dremes, *sb. pl.* dreams, 357.
dresse, 3 *pl. pres. subj.* make ready for, repair to, 290 (O. Fr. *dresser*, Lat. *directus*).
droghte, *sb.* drought, 118.
dul, *adj.* dull, 279.

ebbe, *sb.* ebb-tide, 259.
ech, *adj.* each, every, 299.
eek, *adv.* also, eke, 37, 65, 292.
eft, *adv.* again, 631, 653.
eyled, 3 *s. pret.* ailed, 501.
elles, *adv.* else, otherwise, 118, 209.
enchesoun, *sb.* cause, occasion, 456 (O. Fr. *encheson*, Lat. *occasionem*).

endelong, *adv.* along the length of, 416 (a 13th century word which, acc. to *N.E.D.*, was formed by popular etymology to take the place of *andlang,* the old form of *along*).

enformed, *p.p.* informed, 335.

engyn, *sb.* engine, contrivance, 184 (O. Fr. *engin,* Lat. *ingenium*).

entende, *v.* attend to, 689.

entente, *sb.* meaning, understanding, intention, 107, 400, 521.

er, *adv.* ere, before, 460, 468.

ere, *sb.* ear, 196, 316. '

esily, *adv.* easily, 115.

estat, *sb.* state, 26 (O. Fr. *estat,* Lat. *status*).

ever in oon, always alike, 417.

fable, *sb.* fictitious story, 180.

face, *sb.* astrological face (see note), 50.

fairye, *sb.* fairyland, 96, 201.

fals, *adj.* false, 139.

falsed, *p.p.* falsified, 627.

fantasies, *sb. pl.* fancies, 205.

faste, *adv.* **faste bi,** close by, near, 504.

faucon, *sb.* falcon, 411.

feend, *sb.* enemy, fiend, 522, 602.

feeste, *sb.* feast, 45, 299; **feestes,** *pl.* 219.

feestlych, *adj.* festive, 281.

felawe, *sb.* fellow, companion, 216 (O. E. *felage,* "the primary sense is one who lays down money in a joint undertaking with others," *N.E.D.*).

fer, *adv.* far, 538 (O. E. *feor*).

ferde, 3 *s. pret.* fared, behaved, 461, 621.

ferforth, *adv.* far forward, 567.

fern, *adv.* of old time, 257 (O. E. *fyrn*).

fern-asshen, *sb. pl.* ashes of fern, 254.

festeiynge, *pres. part.* making festival for, entertaining, 345.

fet, *p.p.* fetched, 276 (O. E. *fetian*).

fil, 3 *s. pret.* fell, 473; **fille,** 3 *pl. pret.* 238.

fynally, *adv.* finally, at last, 309.

fleen, *v.* to fly, 122; **fleeth,** 3 *s. pres.* flies, 149.

floures, *sb. pl.* flowers, 512.

foo, *sb.* foe, 136.

for, *conj.* because, 583.

fordrye, *adj.* very dry, 409.

forfered, *p.p.* greatly afraid, 527 (the prefix *for-* gives to an adj. the sense of an absolute superlative, 'very,' 'extremely.' Cp. Lat. *perteritus*).

fortunat, *adj.* fortunate, 25.

fowel, *sb.* fowl, bird, 149; **foweles,** *pl.* 53, 398.

free, *adj.* free-born, noble, 489.

freend, *sb.* friend, 136.

freendly, *adj.* friendly, 274.

fremde, *adj.* foreign, 429 (O. E. *fremede,* Mod. Ger. *fremd*).

fro, *prep.* from, 262.

fruyt, *sb.* fruit, profit, 74.

ful, *adv.* fully, very, 55, 90.

fulsomnesse, *sb.* abundance, fulness, 405.

fumositee, *sb.* vapouriness, 358 ("vapourous humour rising into the head from the stomach," *N.E.D.*).

furial, *adj.* furious, raging, 448.

galoche, *sb.* patten, high shoe, 555 (O. Fr. *galoche,* Low Lat. *galopus,* Gr. καλόπους).

galpynge, *pres. part.* gaping, 350, 354 (not found in O.E.; cognate with *yelp*).

gan, 3 *s. pret.* began (used almost as an auxiliary like 'did'), 262, 348.

gauren, *v.* to gaze, stare, 190 (possibly a frequentative form of obsolete *gau*, of same meaning).

geestes, *sb. pl.* stories 211 (O. Fr. *geste,* Lat. *gesta,* acts, achievements).

gentillesse, *sb.* gentleness, 483.

geten, *p.p.* gotten, 56.

gyn *sb.* contrivance, 128, 322 (cp. *engyn*).

gyse, *sb.* wise, manner, 332, 540 (Fr. *guise*).

glade, *v.* gladden, 634; **gladeth,** 3 *s. pres.*

glas, *sb.* glass, 82, 254.

glood, 3 *s. pret.* glided, 393.

glose, *sb.* gloss, explanation, pretence, 166 (Fr. *glose,* Gr. γλῶσσα).

goodlich, *adv.* goodly, 623.

goon, *v.* to go, 364; **gooth,** 3 *s. pres.* goes, 267, 277, 302; **goon,** *p.p.* gone, 536.

gossomer, *sb.* gossamer, cobweb, 259 (lit. goose-summer or summer-goose down, which appears in summer).

governaunce, *sb.* government, management, 311.

greet, *adj.* great, 13.

greyn, *sb.* grain (of dye), 511.

grene, *sb.* greenness, 54.

grete, *adj.* great, 306.

hadde, 3 *s. pret.* had, 208.

halle-dore, *sb.* hall-door, 80.

halt, 3 *s. pres.* holds, 61.

han, *v.* to have, 56; 3 *pl. pres.* have, 186, 235.

happeth, 3 *s. pres.* happens, 592.

hardyng, *sb.* hardening, 243.

heddes, *sb. pl.* heads, 203, 358.

heed, *sb.* head, 90, 411.

heele, *v.* to heal, 240.

heere, *v.* to hear, 188.

heeste, *sb.* command, 114.

heigh, heighe, *adj.* high, 36, 85, 98.

hem, *pron.* them, 56, 187, 214, 290.

herd, *p.p.* heard, 235, 242.

herknynge, *pres. part.* hearkening, listening to, 78.

heronsewes, *sb. pl.* young herons, 68 (O. Fr. *herounceu*).

herte, *sb.* heart, 120, 212 (O. E. *heorte*).

hertly, *adj.* hearty, 5 (O. E. *heortelich*).

hevene, *sb.* heaven, 149, 271, 558.

hewe, *sb.* hue, complexion, appearance, 508, 587, 640.

hye, *adj.* high, 122, 226 (read of E² for *maistre*), 266, 410; **hyer,** *comp.* higher, 387.

hye, *v.* hurry, 291.

highte, 3 *s. pret.* was called, 30 (from O. E. *haten*).

hym, *pron. dat.* 16.

hir, *poss. adj.* her, 34; **hir, hire,** their, 55, 66, 199, 235, 273.

his, *gen. s.* its, 260.

hit, 3 *s. pres.* hideth, 512.

holde, *p.p.* held, considered, 70.

holpe, *p.p.* helped, 666.

hom, *sb.* home, to home, 635.

hool, *adj.* whole, sound, 161.

hoold, *sb.* hold, grasp, 167.

hoote, *adj.* hot, 51.

hors, *sb.* horse, 181.

horsly, *adj.* belonging or proper to a horse, 194.

Idus, *sb. gen. s.* Ides, the 13th or 15th of the month, 47 (etym. doubtful, see note).

i-knowen, *p.p.* known, 256.

i-seyd, *p.p.* said, 601.

jalouse, *adj.* jealous, 286 (Low Lat. *zelosus,* from Gk. ζῆλος; same origin as *zealous*).

jangle, 3 *pl. pres.* talk idly, wrangle, 220, 261.

janglyng, *sb.* wrangling, idle talking, 258.

jogelours, *sb. pl.* jugglers (O.Fr. *jogleor, jongelor,* Lat. *joculator,* 219).

joly, *adj.* joyous, 48.

jolynesse, *sb.* jollity, mirth, 289.

jolitee, *sb.* jollity, mirth, 278, 344.

jueles, *sb. pl.* jewels, 341.

kan, 1 *s. pres.* can, 4.

keepe, *sb.* heed, care, 348.

kembde, 3 *s. pret.* combed, arranged, 560.

kerve, *v.* to carve, 158.

keste, 3 *s. pret.* kissed, 350.

kynde, *sb.* nature, 610, 619.

kitheth, 3 *s. pres.* shows, 483 (O.E. *cythan*).

knyghtes, *sb. pl.* knights, 69.

knotte, *sb.* knot, entanglement, plot, 401, 407.

knowe, *p.p.* known, 215.

knowen, 3 *pl. pres.* know, 235.

knowyng, *sb.* knowledge, 301.

konnen, 2 *pl. pres.* know, 3.

konnyng, *sb.* knowledge, ability, 35, 251.

koude, 3 *s. pret.* could, 97, 240 ; should know, 39.

lad, *p.p.* led, 172.

laft, *p.p.* left, 186, 263.

lakked, 3 *s. pret.* was lacking to, 16.

large, *adj.* full, complete, 360.

lay, *sb.* law, creed, 18 (O.Fr. *lei, lai=loi,* Lat. *lex*).

ledene, *sb.* tongue, language, 434, 436, 478 (O.E. *laeden,* Lat. *Latinum,* the Latin language, and so language in general).

leere, 3 *pl. pres.* learn, 104.

leeste, *adj.* least, most insignificant, 300.

leet, 3 *s. pret.* let, caused, 45.

leeve, *adj.* beloved, 341 (O.E. *leöf*).

leyde, 3 *s. pret.* laid, 313.

leyser, *sb.* leisure, 493 (O.Fr. *leisir,* Lat. *licere,* to be permitted).

lenger, *adj. comp.* longer, 381, 574.

leste, 3 *s. pres.* it is pleasing to, 125, 380. Cp. **list.**

lete, 1 *s. pres.* leave, 290, 344.

lettre, *sb.* letter, 101.

leve, *sb.* leave, permission, 363.

levere, *adj. comp.* dearer, 572 ; *adv.* rather, 683.

lewed, *adj.* common, vulgar, ignorant, 221.

lewednesse, *sb.* ignorance, 223.

lyche, *adj.* like, 62.

lief, *adj.* dear, 572.

lige, *adj.* liege, lawful, 111.

lighte, *v.* grow light or gay, 396.

lighte, 3 *s. pres.* alights, 169.

lyk, *adj.* like, 207, 255.

list, lyst, 3 *s. pres.* it is pleasing to, 118, 122, 123.

lystes, *sb. pl.* lists, enclosed space for a tournament, 668 (O.Fr. *lisses,* Low Lat. *liciae,* barriers).

lite, litel, *adj.* little, 565, 590.

lith, lyth, 3 *s. pres.* lieth, lies, 322, 474, 35.

lond, *sb.* land, 69.

longynge (for), *pres. part.* belonging to, 39.

lorn, *p.p.* lost, 629.

los, *sb.* loss, 74.

loude, *adv.* loudly, 55.

lowe, *adv.* softly, 216.

lust, *sb.* pleasure, 6, 402.

lustiheed, *sb.* amorous mirth, 288.

lusty, *adj.* pleasant, 52, 158, 272, 389.

maad, *p.p.* made, 222.

maistre, *sb. used adjectivally,* master, chief, 226 (reading of II⁵).

maistresse, *sb.* mistress, duenna, 374 (O.Fr. *maistre,* master, with fem. suffix *-esse*).

maken, *v.* make, 254.

maner, manere, *sb.* manner, kind of, method, 138, 329, 187.

mansioun, *sb.* mansion, astrological house, the sign in which the sun or any planet has its special residence, 50.

marbul, *sb.* marble, 500.

medicynes, *sb. pl.* medicines, 244.

meynee, *sb.* train, retinue, 391 (O.Fr. *mesnee,* as from a Low Lat. *mansionata,* household; cp. *menial*).

mente, 3 *s. pret.* meant, 108.

meridional, *adj.* southern, 263.

merveille, *sb.* marvel, 87; **mervailles,** *pl.* 660.

mesurable, *adj.* temperate, 362.

mete, *sb.* meat, 70, 173.

mewe, *sb.* hawk's cage, 643, 646 (O.Fr. *mue,* a cage where birds are placed to moult, from verb *muer,* Lat. *mutare,* to change).

myn, *poss. adj.* mine, 37.

mynstralcye, *sb.* minstrelsy, music, 268 (Fr. *ménestrel,* Lat. *ministralis,* a servant).

mirour, *sb.* mirror, 143.

mo, *adj.* more, 301.

mooste, *adj.* most, greatest, most important, 199, 300.

moot, 1 *s. pres.* must, 41; **moote, mooten,** 2 *pl. pres.* 161, 316.

morwe, *sb.* morn, morrow, 366.

morwenynge, *sb.* morning, 397.

moste, 3 *s. pres.* must, 38, 280.

muchel, *adj.* much, 349.

namo, no more, 573.

namoore, no more, 314.

nas, ne was, was not, 423.

nat, *adv.* not, 5, 97, 197.

natheles, nathelees, *adv.* nevertheless, 253, 395.

nativitee, *sb.* nativity, birth, 45.

natureel, *adj.* natural, 116.

naturelly, *adv.* naturally, by natural means, 229.

ne, *adv.* and *conj.* not, 86, 97; nor, 68, 197.

neer, *adv. comp.* nearer.

neigh, *adj.* nigh, near, 49; *adv.* nearly, 431.

nempne, *v.* call, name, 318

newefangel, *adj.* fond of novelty, ready to seize (O.E. *fangen*) on what is new, 618.

newefangelnesse, *sb.* fondness of novelty, 610.

nyce, *adj.* foolish, 525 (O.F. *nice,* Lat. *nescius,* ignorant)

nyn, ne in, nor in, 35.

nys, ne is, is not, 72, 255, 359.

nyste, 3 *pl. pret.* **ne wiste,** knew not, 502, 634.

nobleye, *sb.* nobility, dignity, state, 77.

nolde, ne wolde, would not, 421.

noon, *adj.* none, 41.

noot, ne woot, know not, 342.

norice, *sb.* nurse, 347 (Fr. *nourice,* Lat. *nutrix*).

novelries, *sb. pl.* novelties, 619 (O.Fr. *novelrie*).

now and now, *adv. phrase,* from time to time, 430.

o, *num. adj.* one, 116, 581.

obeisaunce, *sb.* obeisance, marks of respect, submissiveness, 93, 562.

ook, *s.b.* oak, 159.

oon, *num. adj.* one, 212.

operacioun, *sb.* operation, task, 130.

ordeyned, *p.p.* ordained, 177.

ordre, *sb.* order, 62, 92.

outher, *conj.* either, 420, 455.
over, *prep.* besides, 137.

pace, *v.* pass, go, 120; 1 *s. pres.
subj.* pass away, 494.
paleys, *sb.* palace, 60.
parementz, *sb. pl.* rich array,
decorations (O.Fr. *parement,*
Low Lat. *paramentum,* 269).
pas, *sb.* pace, **a pas,** at a foot
pace, 388.
passe of, pass over, 288 (*var.*)./
peynes, *sb. pl.* pains, 480.
peple, *sb.* people, 220, 252.
percen, *v.* pierce, 237.
peregryn, *adj.* foreign, migra-
tory, pilgrim, 428 (Lat. *pere-
grinus*).
pyes, *sb. pl.* magpies, 649 (Fr.
pie, Lat. *pica*).
pyn, *sb.* pin, 316, 328.
pyne, *sb.* pain, 448.
pitous, *adj.* piteous, 412.
pitously, *adv.* piteously, 414.
plat, *sb.* flat side, 162.
platte, *adj.* flat, 164 (Fr. *plat,*
Ger. *platt*).
pleye, *v.* play, 78; **pleyen,** 3
pl. pres. 219.
pleyn, *adv.* plainly, 151.
plesance, *sb.* pleasant manners,
509 (O.Fr. *plaisance,* Low
Lat. *placentia*).
Poilleys, *adj.* Apulian, 195.
point-devys, at, carefully, to a
nicety, 560.
polyve, *sb.* pulley, 184.
prees, *sb.* press, crowd, 189.
preyede, 3 *s. pret.* prayed, 311.
presentes, *sb. pl.* gifts, 174.
preved, *p.p.* proved, 481.
prighte, 3 *s. pret.* pricked, 418.
pryme, *sb.* the first hour or first
quarter of the day, so the time
between 6 and 9 a.m., 73;
pryme large, full prime, 9
o'clock.
privee, *adj.* privy, secret, 531.

proces, *sb.* process, course, 658.
prolixitee, *sb.* prolixity, long-
windedness, 405.
proporcioned, *p.p.* proportioned,
fashioned, 191.
propre, *adj.* proper, 619.
prospectives, *sb. pl.* perspective
glasses, telescopes, 234.
purs, *sb.* purse, 148.

queynte, *adj.* curious, 234, 239,
360 (O.Fr. *coint.* Lat. *cog-
nitus*).
quyk, *adj.* quick, lively, 194
(O.E. *cwic*).
quod, 3 *s. pret.* quoth, said, 212,
449.

ravysshed, *p.p.* carried away,
547.
rebelle, *v.* rebell, 5.
recche, 3 *pl. pres.* think, con-
sider, 71.
recours, *sb.* recourse, return, 75.
rede, *adj.* red, 415.
rede, *v.* read, 211.
redy, *adj.* 114.
reflexiouns, *sb. pl.* reflections,
230.
regioun, *sb.* region, land, 14.
regne, *sb.* kingdom, 135 (Lat.
regnum).
rehercen, *v.* rehearse, relate,
298.
reyne, *sb.* rein, 313.
renewed, *p.p.* removed, 181 (Fr.
remuer).
renneth, 3 *s. pres.* runs, 479.
renoun, *sb.* renown, fair fame,
13, 530.
repaire, *v.* repair, come to, 589;
repeireth, 3 *s. pres.* 339;
repeirynge, *pres. part.* 608.
reson, *sb.* reason, cause, 296.
resouned, 3 *s. pret.* resounded,
413.
rethor, *sb.* master of rhetoric, 38.
ryche, *adj.* rich, 61.

richely, *adv.* richly, 90.
right, *adv.* thoroughly, 215.
roche, *sb.* rock, 500 (Fr. *roche*).
rody, *adj.* ruddy, rosy, 385, 394.
roial, *adj.* royal, 26, 264.
ronne, *p.p.* run, 386.
roos, 3 *s. pret.* rose, 266.
route, *sb.* assembly, procession, 303, 382 (O.Fr. *route*, Low Lat. *rota, rupta*).
routhe, *sb.* ruth, pity, 438.
rowned, 3 *s. pret.* rounded, whispered, 216 (O.E. *rūnian*; for the later addition of *d*, cp. *soun* and *sound*).

saleweth, 3 *s. pres.* salutes, 91, 112 (Fr. *saluer*, Lat. *saluare*).
saugh, 1 *s. pret.* saw, 460.
save, *prep.* except, 90 (Fr. *sauf*, Lat. *salvus*).
secte, *sb.* sect, school of religion, 17.
seel, *sb.* seal, 131 (O.Fr. *seel*, Lat. *sigillum*).
seen, *v.* see, 303, 513.
sege, *sb.* siege, 306.
sey, 1 *s. pres.* say, 289; 2 *s. imper.* 2; seiden, seyden, 3 *pl. pret.* 231, 253; seyn, 3 *pl. pret.* 252; seyn, *inf.* to say, 117, 163, 314, 434; seith, 3 *s. pres.* 99 (*var*).
semblant, *sb.* appearance, 516.
semed, 3 *s. pret.* it seemed to, 56.
served, 3 *s. pret.* preserved, concealed, 521.
servyse, *sb.* service, 66, 280.
sesoun, *sb.* season, 54, 389, 397.
seten, 3 *pl. pres.* sit, 92.
seuretee, *sb.* surety, assurance, 528 (O.Fr. *seurté*, Lat. *securitas*).
sewes, *sb. pl.* dishes, 67 (O.E. *seaw*).
shapen, 3 *pl. pres.* dispose, 214.
sheene, *adj.* bright, 53 (O.E. *scēne*, Ger. *schön*).

sholde, 3 *s.* should, 102, 245.
shoon, 3 *s. pret.* shone, 170.
shoures, *sb. pl.* showers, 118.
shrighte, 3 *s. pret.* from *schrichen*, shrieked, 417, 422.
shul, 3 *s.* shall, 357.
syde, *sb.* side, 84.
signe, *sb.* astrological sign (see note), 51.
syk, *sb.* sigh, 498 (O.E. *sīcan*, to sigh).
sikerly, *adv.* surely, assuredly, 180 (Lat. *securus*).
sllable, *sb.* syllable, 101 (O.Fr. *sillable, sillabe*, Gk. συλλαβή. The last *l* is excrescent).
similitude, *sb.* likeness, 480.
syn, *adv.* since, 306, 457.
sit, 3 *s. pres.* sits, 77, 179.
skiles, *sb. pl.* reasons, arguments, 205 (O. Norse, *skil*).
sle, 2 *pl. pres.* slay, 462 (O.E. *slēan*, to kill).
slye, *adj.* clever, 230 (O. Norse, *slœgr*).
smerte, *adj.* smart, pricking, 480.
smerte, 3 *s. pres. subj.* hurt, 564.
snybbed, *p.p.* reproved, 688.
sodeynly, *adv.* suddenly, 80, 89, 625.
solempne, *adj.* solemn, famous, 61, 111.
solempnely, *adv.* solemnly, 179.
som, *pl.* some, 213.
someres, *sb. gen.* summer's, 64, 142.
sondry, *adj.* sundry, various, 220, 243.
sones, *sb. pl.* sons, 29.
songen, 3 *pl. pret.* sang, 55.
sonne, *sb.* sun, 53, 385.
soore, *v.* soar, 123.
soore, *adv.* sorely, 258.
soote, *adj.* sweet, 389.
sooth, *adj.* true, 21.
soper, *sb.* supper, 290.

sophymes, *sb. pl.* sophisms, delusions, 554 (Gk. σόφισμα).

sorwe, *sb.* sorrow, 422.

sorwful, *adj.* sorrowful, 585.

soupen, 3 *pl. pres.* sup, 297.

sowne, *v.* sound, 105 ; **sownen**, 3 *pl. pres.* 270 ; **sowneth into**, 3 *pl.* belong to, 517 (Lat. *sonare*).

speche, *sb.* speech, oratory, 94, 104.

speeke, speken, 3 *pl. pres.* speak, 247, 232, 243.

spere, *sb.* spear, 239.

stant, 3 *s. pres.* stands, 171, 182, 316.

stevene, *sb.* voice, speech, 150 (O. E. *stefn*).

stile, *sb.* style, method of speaking or writing, 105 (Lat. *stilus*).

style, *sb.* stepping-place over a fence, 106 (O. E. *stigel*).

styward, *sb.* steward, 291 (lit. warden or keeper of a *sty*).

stondeth, 3 *s. pres.* stands, 190.

stoon, *sb.* stone, 171.

strawe, 2 *s. pres. subj.* strew, 613.

strook, *sb.* stroke, 160.

subtiltee, *sb.* subtlety, craft, 140 (Lat. *subtilitas*).

swannes, *sb. pl.* swans, 68.

swerd, *sb.* sword, 57.

swich, *adj.* such, 27, 41, 157, 215.

swowneth, 3 *s. pres.* swoons, faints, 430.

take, *p.p.* taken, 363.

taryen, *v.* cause to tarry, delay, 73.

Tartre, *adj.* Tartar, 266.

tercelet, *sb.* "the male of any kind of hawk ; so termed because he is commonly a third part less than the female" (Cotgreave), 504.

thanne, *adv.* then, 64.

tharray, the array, 63.

theffect, the effect, the effectual part, 322.

thennes, *adv.* thence, 326.

ther, *adv.* where, 179.

ther as, *adv.* where, 267, 270, 306.

ther-inne, *adv.* therein, 213.

ther-with, *adv.* therewith, thereto, moreover, 194.

therwithal, *adv.* thereto, in addition, 244.

thikke, *adj.* thick, 159.

thilke, the ilk, the same, 162, 607.

thynges, *sb. pl.* musical compositions, 78 (see note).

thise, *dem. pron. pl.* these, 211.

tho, *adv.* then, 308.

thombe, *sb.* thumb, 83.

thonder, *sb.* thunder, 258.

thoughte, 3 *s. pret.* it seemed to, 527.

thridde, *adj.* third, 76.

thurgh, *prep.* through, 11, 121.

thurghout, *prep.* throughout, 158.

tyde, *sb.* tide, season, 142.

tidives, *sb. pl.* small birds, 648.

til, *adv.* till, 269.

to, *adv.* too, 525.

toforn, *prep.* before, 268.

tonge, *sb.* tongue, 35.

tour, *sb.* tower, 176 (Fr. *tour*, Lat. *turris*).

trench, *sb.* cutting, 392.

tresoun, *sb.* treason, 139 (O. Fr. *traison*, Lat. acc. *traditionem*).

trete, 3 *pl. pres.* discuss, 219.

trille, *v.* turn, twist, 316; 2 *s. imperat.* 321, 328.

trippe, *v.* trip, skip, 312.

trone, *sb.* throne, 275.

trowe, 1 *s. pres.* trow, believe, 213.

twynne, *v.* depart, 577.
twiste, *sb.* branch, 442.
twiste, *v.* twist, wring, 566.

unbokele, *v.* unbuckle, 555.
understonde, *p.p.* understood, 437.
unfeestlich, *adv.* unfestive, 366.
unknowe, *adj.* unknown, 246.
unkouthe, *adj.* strange, unknown, 284.
usshers, *sb. pl.* ushers, attendants, 293.

veluettes, *sb. pl.* velvets, 644.
verray, *adj.* true, genuine, 166.
verraily, *adv.* verily, truly, 466.
vertu, *sb.* virtue, property, special quality, 146, 157, 310, 593.
vestiment, *sb.* array, clothing, 59.
vice, *sb.* fault, 101.
voyden, *v.* remove, 188.
voys, *sb.* voice, 99, 412.

wayten, *v.* await, watch, 443; 3 *pl. pres.* 88; wayted, 3 *s. pret.* watched.
wan, 3 *s. pret.* won, 662, 664.
war, *adj.* aware, wary, 490.
weder, *sb.* weather, 52.
weel, *adv.* well, 115.
welle, *sb.* well, fountain, 505.
wem, *sb.* spot, blemish, 121.
wend, *p.p.* thought, 510; wende, 3 *pl. pret.* 198.
wende, 3 *pl. pres.* go, 296; went, *p.p.* 567.
werreyed, 3 *s. pret.* warred against, 10.
whan, whanne, *adv.* when, 168, 245.
wher, *conj.* whether, 579
wher-so, *adv.* wheresoever, 118.
whider, *adv.* whither, 378.

whil, *adv.* while, 167.
whit, *adj.* white, 409.
wyf, *sb.* wife, 29.
wight, *sb.* man, creature, 138, 329, 355, 457, 557.
wyl, *sb.* will, 5.
wilneth, 3 *s. pres.* desires, 120.
wyn, *sb.* wine, 292.
wyndas, *sb.* windlass, 184.
wynne, *v.* win, gain, 214.
wynter, *pl.* winters, 43.
wys, *adj.* wise, 559.
wise, *sb.* manner, 521.
wisly, *adv.* surely, certainly, 469.
wyst, *p.p.* wist, known, 260;
wiste, 3 *s. pret.* knew, 399.
withouten, *prep.* without, 121, 180.
wittes, *sb. pl.* wits, imaginations, 203.
wode, *sb.* wood, 413.
wol, 1 *s. pres.* will, 4.
wolde, 3 *s.* would, 237.
wonder, *adj.* wondrous, 248, 254.
wondred, 3 *pl. pret.* wondered, 307.
wondren, 3 *pl. pres.* wonder, 258.
wondryng, *verb. sub.* wondering, 305, 308.
woot, 3 *s. pres.* knows, 299; 2 *pl. pres.* 519.
wopen, *p.p.* wept, 523.
wreke, 2 *pl. pres.* avenge, 454.
writen, 3 *pl. pret.* wrote, 233.
withyng, *sb.* twisting, 127.
wroghte, 3 *s. pret.* wrought, made, 128.

yaf, 1 *s. pret.* gave, 533; 3 *s. pres.* 542.
y-beten, *p.p.* beaten, 414.
y-bore, y-born, *p.p.* born, carried, 326, 340.
y-drawe, *p.p.* drawn, 326.

yeve, 2 s. *pres. subj.* give, 614.
yeven, *p.p.* given, 541.
y-fet, *p.p.* fetched, 174.
y-fynde, *v.* find, 470.
y-glewed, *p.p.* glued, fastened, 182.
y-goon, *p.p.* gone, 293, 538.
y-harded, *p.p.* hardened, 245.
yliche, *adj.* alike, 20.
y-maad, *p.p.* made, 218.
ynowe, *adj.* enough, 470.

yong, yonge, *adj.* young, 23, 55, 385; **yonge,** *pl.* young people, 88; **yongest,** *sup.* 33.
yoore, *adv.* a long time, 403.
yow, *pron.* you, 73.
ypocrite, *sb.* hypocrite, 520.
y-quit, *p.p.* acquitted, 673.
y-rekened, *p.p.* reckoned, 427.
y-set, *p.p.* set, 173.
y-swore, *p.p.* sworn, 325.
y-toold, *p.p.* told, 357.

GLASGOW: PRINTED AT THE UNIVERSITY PRESS BY ROBERT MACLEHOSE AND CO.